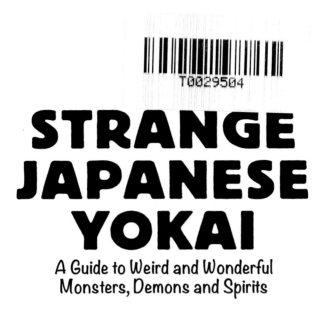

STRANGE JAPANESE YOKAI

A Guide to Weird and Wonderful
Monsters, Demons and Spirits

Kenji Murakami

Translated by **Zack Davisson**

TUTTLE Publishing

Tokyo | Rutland, Vermont | Singapore

Contents

Introduction

Yokai have a reputation as creatures of horror, but this is not true of all of them. Certainly, there are many scary Yokai—killers and human-eating monsters—but that is only one type among an endless variety. There are just as many that are cute or silly—or downright stupid. For this collection I have assembled only the most unusual Yokai, the weirdest of the bunch. Some are well-known, others are obscure; the one thing they share in common is that they are guaranteed to disappoint (if you were expecting them to be scary). Please enjoy this pantheon of the pathetic, this bestiary of the broken.

—**Kenji Murakami**

A Note About the Book

This book was written to get people interested in Japanese culture through Yokai. Some of the Yokai here are vulgar, some are stupid—and some are even charming—but understand that every monster here, no matter how disgusting, is part of the cultural legacy created and inherited by the Japanese. For a long time Yokai were only seriously studied by what we might call enthusists, but in recent years they have gained attention in academic fields. Interest in Yokai is nothing to be embarrassed about. It's actually a lot of fun! We hope this book helps people get interested in the lives and beliefs of those who came before them, as well as the history and legends of Japan.

Guide to Symbols

◊ = Haunting area   ▌ = Reference material

❈ = Appearance era   ✎ = Note

The haunting areas are listed using modern names of cities, towns, and villages to make them easier to understand. Some of the older stories are listed as "A tale from region XXX." When a question mark is in "Appearance era" it means the date is unknown. For detailed reference material, see the references at the end of the book.

Say "Yokai" and what springs to mind? Oni. Kappa. Kitsune. Tengu. These are the superstars of Japan's Yokai. Yet even among their lofty ranks are some that are pitiful.

CHAPTER

Yokai Superstars

Oni

Surprising!
A monstrous Oni with
elegant tastes!

Do Oni appreciate music and theater?

Since ancient times, Oni have been portrayed as ugly and frightening. They eat people, commit all sorts of violence, and spread infectious diseases. In short, they terrorize humans. Yet in the Heian period, in the capital of Kyoto, there were Oni who enjoyed playing musical instruments and composing poetry.

Data File

⚲ Kyoto, Kyoto prefecture ❉ Heian period

▯ *Animal Yokai Collection*, Vol. 1

✎ Rashomon was the main gate to Kyoto, the Heian-period capital of Japan. The Rashomon was a large, two-story building that eventually fell into disuse and disrepair. Bandits and Oni were rumored to occupy the second floor.

The *Konjaku Monogatari Shu* (*Record of Ancient Matters*) tells the story of master musician Minamoto no Hiromasa. He was enchanted listening to the music of an Oni playing a biwa. The biwa was named Genjo, a famous instrument from the Imperial treasure house. The Oni stole it and played it on the second floor of the Rashomon Gate. Now, I don't know if this is the same Oni, but the poet Miyako no Yoshiko wrote of a similar strange encounter in his book *Edansho*. He was passing the Rashomon Gate and recited a line from a Chinese poem in appreciation of Spring. An Oni hiding on the second floor was moved and responded with the answering verse. While most Oni are somewhat rough and crude, surely if they are capable of playing musical instruments, they are able to appreciate poetry.

Oni who were tricked!

Oni are so powerful they can hoist massive boulders over their heads. There are several legends where they were said to have hewn ninety-nine stone steps into the sides of mountains. This story was handed down in Bungotakada, Oita prefecture.

A cohort of cannibalistic Oni lived up in the mountains. The villagers below lived in fear and prayed to their local Kami (Shinto god). Hearing their pleas, the Kami appeared before the Oni and issued them a challenge. "If you can carve a hundred steps of stone in the mountain overnight, you can stay and eat all the people you want. If you can't, you must depart."

The Oni knew they were no match for the powerful god. They desperately began to hew the stone and carve the steps. They worked through the night and had finished ninety-nine steps before the approach of day. Stunned at such speed, the Kami imitated the cry of a rooster. Thinking dawn had come and they failed, the Oni grudgingly trudged down the mountain and were never seen again.

They may have been human-eating monsters, but they were tricked so I feel a little sorry for them.

Data File

⚲ Bungotakada, Oita prefecture   ✷ Pre-Heian period?

📖 *Legends of Oita*, Vol. 1

✎ Well-known stories of stone steps made by Oni include the nine hundred and ninety-nine steps at Agagami Shrine Goshado in Oga, Akita prefecture, and the Oni Stairs of Kumano magaibutsu in Bungotakada, Oita prefecture.

Surprising!
Oni that are easily fooled!

Are Oni foolish?

An old tale is told in Gunma prefecture called "Oni and Nagaimo Potato." One day an Oni came down from the mountain to eat some humans. Stumbling across a human house, he peeked inside and saw them grating Oni horn for their dinner. Shocked, the Oni fled, thinking "I came to eat but instead will be eaten!" What the monster thought was an Oni horn was actually an ordinary nagaimo potato. Although not so extreme, there are many such comedic tales of foolish Oni across Japan. Oni are portrayed as naive and easily fooled.

Perhaps the most representative tale of a foolish Oni is the most famous Oni legend of all. The Oni king Shuten-doji lived with his band on Mt. Oe. The warrior Minamoto no Yorimitsu and his famed Four Heavenly Generals journeyed to Mt. Oe to end the menace of Shuten-doji. Disguising themselves as priests on a pilgrimage, they entered Shuten-doji's cave and ate and drank with him. When Shuten-doji was drunk, they cut off his head. When even the king of the Oni can be so careless, is it any wonder the rest of them are no better?

Data File

◊ Throughout Japan   ※ Heian period?

▣ *Joshu Folktales*

✎ Shuten-doji lived in Mt. Oe, in the northern area of Kyoto prefecture. He loved to drink and would often lead raids to kidnap humans to use as servants or to kill and eat.

Surprising!
Stupid Oni fooling themselves!

Kappa

Making the same mistake over and over!

Kappa are aquatic Yokai. Their appearance varies slightly by region, but they are about the size of a human child with a bowl-shaped head surrounded by a bobbed fringe. Some have beaked mouths and shells on their backs. There are old regional names as well, but nowadays they are all called Kappa.

- ○ Throughout Japan
- ❀ Ancient to present
- 📖 *Kappa Folklore Dictionary*
- ✎ Kappa often drag humans into the water to pull shirikodama (a mythical internal organ often thought to be the liver) out of their rears. This kills their victim, and the Kappa eat the shirikodama.

Surprising!

So many Kappa always falling for the same old trick!

No matter what they look like or what they are called, one thing is always true of the Kappa—they love to cause trouble. And most of the time, this trouble comes back to bite them. For example, in several stories they pull humans, cows, and even horses into the water.

Once in the water, they try to grab their victim's butt only to find their hands cut off with a swift knife. Beaten and punished, the Kappa promises to cause no more trouble. In exchange for their life or the return of their hands, they teach their attackers the ways of medicine. Every Kappa makes the same mistake. They inevitably pay for their own mischief, and rarely get what they are after.

Kappa who lose their bowls.

Kappa heads are concave like a bowl and filled with water. Nothing is more important to a Kappa. This water is the key to their strength and if it empties out, they quickly lose their power.

Speaking of bowls, there is a story told in Taito, Tokyo. Around Kuramae, there was a pond in which dwelled a Kappa. A farmer went fishing there one day and caught the Kappa's bowl. He took the bowl home. That night, he heard the Kappa's voice throughout the house, saying "Put it back! Put it back!"

Surprising!
A Kappa who has its bowl fished off its head!

Data File

📍 Kuramae, Taito, Tokyo   ☀ Edo period?

📖 *Folk Tales of Ueno and Asakusa*

🖊 A legend tells of a Kappa in a pond in Kuramae who had his bowl stolen. It was called the Keikebori, or "Leave it behind pond." This is not to be confused with the Keikebori that is one of the Seven Wonders of Honjo.

Surprising!
A Kappa afraid of a plow that looks like a monster!

Data File

📍 Kumamoto prefecture, Yamaga city, Kamotomachi koyanagi

🎏 Edo period   📖 *Kappa Folklore Dictionary*

🖊 A Kappa was supposedly scared of an ordinary plow hauled by cows and horses used in rice fields.

Afraid of being cursed, the farmer returned the bowl to the pond. Legend says that the voice then ceased. This is a strange story because normally a Kappa will die without its bowl. But perhaps this one was different? In any case, without its bowl it was considerably weakened. That's why it could only scare the farmer with its voice.

Scared of an ordinary plow?

Kappa also have things they are afraid of. They don't like gourds, human spit, or rice that has been served before a Buddhist altar. But most of all they hate farming implements.

A long time ago, two brothers lived near the Kikuchi River. One night a Kappa appeared in their dreams. It said, "I live in Senryu Pool, but recently a nine-fanged monster has taken up residence at the entrance to my nest. I'm too scared to go in. Please help me by getting rid of it." When the brothers awoke, they went to the pool and found a plow with nine teeth caught at the entrance of a hole. To the brothers it was an ordinary plow, but to the Kappa it looked like a monster. After the brothers removed the plow, it's said that Kappa never again troubled any of the people in that land.

Kappa are shameless. They play all sorts of tricks on humans but come begging for help whenever they are in trouble.

Kitsune and Tanuki

Who is the better shape shifter?

Kitsune and Tanuki love to prank humans by changing their appearances and casting illusions. As both are similar, they tend to be jealous rivals. They sometimes battle to see who is the most adept shape shifters are.

Once, a Tanuki challenged a Kitsune to a contest of supernatural powers. The Kitsune transformed first into a feast and then into a wedding procession. Suitably impressed, the Tanuki then took its turn.

Surprising!
Killed in a shape
shifting battle!

Data File

⚲ Throughout Japan   ✻ Edo period

📖 *Japanese mukashi banashi Collection*

✍ In the Edo period, regional lords called daimyo were required to journey back
and forth to the capital of Edo (Tokyo). They traveled in grand processions.
Failure to give way when the procession passed was punishable by death.

The Tanuki said he would transform into an entire Daimyo
procession. He asked the Kitsune to transform into a human and
wait around the bend of the road. That way, the Tanuki said, he
could take in the entire, magnificent sight. Doing as it was asked,
the Kitsune was astounded when the procession rounded the
corner. He leapt in front of the procession and shouted "Wow!
What a display! You look like the real thing!"

In an instant, a Samurai of the procession drew his sword and
decapitated the insolent Kitsune. In fact, this was a real procession
that the Tanuki knew was coming.

There are similar stories across Japan. Each region has its
own famous story of Kitsune and Tanuki. In some regions, it's the
Kitsune who deceives the Tanuki. No matter the winner, the
Kitsune and Tanuki are evenly matched in shape shifting powers.

Food used as a trap.

Some Kitsune disguise themselves as humans and work in castles. One of these famous Kitsunes was Yojiro, who served Lord Satake of Kubota Castle, also called Akita Castle. Yojiro worked as a messenger and was able to deliver letters and packages back and forth between Akita and Tokyo with a speed impossible for humans to achieve. However, one day on his way to Tokyo, Yojiro was caught in a trap set in a field.

The trap was set with a Kitsune's favorite food, deep-fried mouse. Yojiro knew he didn't have time to waste, but once the fragrant smell hit his nostrils he could not resist. Even though some part of him knew it was a trap he leapt at the delicious morsel. As he bit into the mouse, Yojiro was killed by a hunter.

Interestingly, Yojiro was not the only Kitsune to fall for this trap. Keizobo of Tottori Castle who also served his lord as a messenger was tempted by a deep-fried mouse trap and killed.

Both Kitsune were intelligent and resolute individuals, but at the end of the day they were still just animals. They could not resist the temptation of their own appetites.

Surprising!
Kitsune who are unable to resist tasty treats!

Data File

♀ Akita, Akita prefecture　　❀ Edo period

▥ *Legends of Murayama Region of Yamagata Prefecture*

✎ In Senshu Park in Akita, there is an Inari shine dedicated to Yojiro. It was built by a lord who felt pity for the Kitsune. There is also a shrine in Higashine, Yamagata prefecture, where it is said that Yojiro was killed.

Shape shifters betrayed by their own appetites.

In the ancient capital of Kamakura, there's a temple called Kencho-ji. A tale is told that the Sanmon Gate, or Mountain Gate, was broken and left unrepaired for some time. In thanks for having been left to live in peace for so long, the Tanuki who lived in the mountains behind Kencho-ji decided to raise funds to repair the structure. The Tanuki transformed to resemble monks from the temple and set out across Japan begging for donations. One went as far as Nirasaki city, in Yamanashi prefecture near Yokohama.

However, no matter how skillful their transformation, a whiff of food revealed their animal natures. When served, the Tanuki monks threw down their chopsticks and stuck their faces directly into their dinners to eat.

Data File

⚲ Kanto Koshinetsu region   ❊ Edo period   📖 *Legends of Kanagawa*

🖌 Kencho-ji is typical of temples located in Kita-Kamakura, Kamakura, Kanagawa prefecture. The main gate, called the Sanmon, is particularly grand. As legend has it, funds for its construction were collected by a tanuki, thus it is called the Tanuki Gate.

Even though the Kencho-ji Tanuki were revealed, the money they collected was used to rebuild the Sanmon Gate. Many were not so lucky. Tales are told of shape-shifted Tanuki who stopped at inns. Unable to maintain concentration in the presence of food, they reverted to their true forms and were killed, just like the Kitsune Yojiro. It seems both Kitsune and Tanuki remain wild beasts at heart and are unable to control themselves around food.

Surprising!
A Tanuki that has no self control!

Tengu

Were Tengu originally weak?

Tengu are Yokai who live in the mountains all across Japan. They possess myriad magical abilities and cause constant mischief for humanity. There are two types of Tengu: bird-faced creatures called Karasu Tengu and red-faced goblins with long noses called Hanataka Tengu.

From the backs of both sprout a pair of wings which they use to fly. Tengu have mercurial personalities. They are kind and helpful to those they like but will just as quickly lash out and kill those they don't. Originally, Tengu were formless mountain spirits. When they appeared to people, they took the form of birds called black kites.

A novice Tengu who can't manage to get revenge!

Data File

◊ Throughout Japan ☀ Ancient to modern times ▯ *Tengu!*

✎ The trouble caused by tengu varies from surprising mountain hikers, to hindering monks on pilgrimages, to causing society-disrupting plagues and disasters.

A story in the *Konjaku Monogatari shu* (*Tales of Times Past*) tells of a Tengu appearing in a persimmon tree, taking the appearance of a shining Buddha. A government official glared suspiciously at the apparition. This was enough to break the spell. The Tengu fell from the tree and tumbled to the ground, reverting to its true form, a common kestrel.

In other tales, Tengu take the form of buzzards that can be killed even by children. Tengu first appeared in stories like these as powerless Yokai. Over the years, they developed supernatural abilities and evolved into Karasu and Hanataka Tengu.

Freshly cooked rice that is too hot to handle!

Some workers have to travel up to the mountains. These workers

are often met there by Tengu waiting to play jokes on them. A rain of pebbles falling from the sky, or the sound of a tree falling when there is none to be found, are accompanied by the cackling sound of a Tengu's laughter. This sort of practical joke appeals to the Tengu's sense of humor.

There are stories like this told of Mt. Hataka in Gunma prefecture. Many woodcutters shared a hut in Mt. Hataka where they would spend the night after an exhausting day of logging.

One day the cook was boiling rice is a massive pot. Without warning, a huge hand thrust down from the ceiling and plunged into the pot, grabbing a fistful of rice. It was so hot it burned! The hand spasmed in pain, flinging rice all over the hut. This was a Tengu trying to steal rice. It probably used its magic to enlarge its hand, thinking it could grab all the rice at once and gobble it up.

Surprising!
A Tengu burning its own hand while stealing rice!

The Tengu that was sick of mountain life.

This is a Tengu tale from Odake, Nobeoka in Miyazaki prefecture. Long ago there was a temple called Otake-ji. One night a young traveling monk arrived, asking to stay the night. The master prepared a meal and a bed for the traveler.

Data File

⚲ Minakami, Tone, Gunma prefecture   ❅ Beginning Edo-Showa period?

📕 *Kitsune's Yawn: Folktales of Fujiwara*

📝 There's a hut on Mt. Hataka called Hut of the Hand which is named after this legend. It's also said that the rice scattered around by the giant hand smelled so disgusting no one could eat it.

The next day the traveling monk tended the temple garden as thanks. The Master was so pleased he invited the young monk to stay. The monk was overjoyed and worked diligently every day.

Surprising!
A Tengu skipping out on ascetic training!

Data File

📍 Odake, Nobeoka, Miyazaki prefecture ☀ Edo period?

📖 *Legends of Miyazaki*

✒ Tengu hold a feathered fan with which is it said they can control the wind and fire. Because of this, Tengu may be worshiped as deities of fire prevention.

However, it seemed the boy worked a little too fast. Even when assigned a task far away, he would be back in the blink of an eye, napping against an old tree. The traveling monk was soon revealed to be a Tengu. The Tengu, it seemed, was sick of ascetic training in the mountains and decided that a nice relaxing temple life was the thing for him.

The Tengu took to the skies, saying "With my true form revealed I can no longer stay here, but in thanks for your kindness this temple shall never know fire." Otake-ji claims this is the origin of Bicho Boson, a Buddhist guardian deity enshrined there that provides protection from fire. This kind of Tengu is rare.

Yokai Origins 1

Mukashi Banashi Fairy Tales

Traditional stories passed down and enjoyed for many generations are called folktales. Within that broad category there are assorted styles, like legendary stories, urban legends and fairy tales. Yokai can appear differently depending on the style of the story. Fairy tales, called Mukashi Banashi, (tales from long ago), usually begin with "Once upon a time..." There is rarely a specified time or place given and storylines follow common patterns. Of course, there are always exceptions. It can be complicated....

Generally speaking, Mukashi Banashi are told by adults to children. They can be funny and a little strange and many are very witty. In Mukashi Banashi, the Yokai are rarely scary. They tend to be foolish and easily defeated.

Yokai behavior is often incomprehensible. It is sometimes even comedic. Why they act like that is a mystery only the Yokai themselves know.

2

Outrageous Yokai

Akadenchu

Only cute trouble allowed!

Everyone knows there is a large population of magic Tanuki called Bakedanuki in Tokushima prefecture on Shikoku Island. An accurate count has never been made but it is safe to say there are hundreds. There are two species; the Bakedanuki which are the same size as regular Tanuki; and smaller ones called Mamedanuki.

The only difference is in their size. Their supernatural abilities are the same, as is their love of annoying humans. Tokushima Mamedanuki's pranks are mostly harmless and silly.

Take for example Akadenchu, a Mamedanuki who lives in Naruto city. Akadenchu shapeshifts into the form of a child wearing a sleeveless red *haori* coat. He appears to people walking home at night and asks for a piggyback ride. If refused, Akadenchu cries and begs and follows the person, annoying them until they give in. If given a piggyback ride, he squeals with delight and lightly drums on the person's back in excitement.

That's it. That is all Akadenchu does. Its mischievous, yes, but at the same time endearing. It makes you want to give him a piggyback ride.

Surprising!
Bakedanuki are too cute for words!

Data File

📍 Otani, Oasa, Naruto, Tokushima prefecture　　☀ Beginning Showa period?

📖 *Tanuki Tales of Awa*

✍ Akadenchu wears a sleeveless haori coat called a *denchu*. They are similar to *chanchanko* vests. In western Japan these are called *denchi*.

Amagozen

A female Kappa leader from the Heike clan!

Amagozen is a female Kappa from Fukuoka prefecture. Formerly human, she was the wife of Heike general Notonokami Noritsune. In the Heian period, the Genji and Heike clans fought the Genpei War, waging the decisive battle at Dan-no-ura. The Heike lost.

Noritsune was slain and fell into the ocean. His wife and her handmaid flung themselves into the waves while cursing the Genji clan. They were reborn as Kappa, swimming the ocean near Kyushu Island. They only attacked members of the Genji clan.

Surprising!
A powerful Kappa afraid of flowers!

Amagozen takes a break from her revenge every May 5. She will say "I will only come back when the buckwheat flowers are no longer in bloom" and then retreats into her home. Amagozen despises buckwheat flowers because the white color and pattern reminds her of the hated Genji clan crest. Inside her dwelling, she trembles in fear while her servants care for her and wait for the flowers to stop blooming.

Amagozen is normally a powerful leader, but when the buckwheat flowers bloom, she is a pitiful sight!

Data File

◊ Kitakyushu, Munakata, Fukuoka prefecture   ※ Beginning Showa period?

▪ *Kappa Monogatari*

∥ Dan-no-ura sits off the Kanmon Straight on the border between Yamaguchi prefecture and Fukuoka prefecture. It is famous as being the location of the last battle of the Genpei War between the Heike and Genji clans.

Okonjoro

A magical fox that tries to be helpful!

Jomyo-ji is a temple in Kasaichi, Higashi, Hamamatsu in Shizuoka prefecture. In the past, a Bakegitsune (a magical fox) called Okonjoro lived in the thick forests that surrounded the temple. Her name means "Blue Woman," named after the dark blue kimono she wore when appearing before humans, shapeshifting into a beautiful woman.

She never caused trouble, only assisting at the temple, or helping neighbors when needed. She was especially observant of when the temple needed anything and would take the initiative of ordering from shops. However, once Okonjoro made a mistake by ordering eye medicine from the local pharmacy.

The Abbot of the temple had said that he had a boil on his backside, but he couldn't see it very well to treat it. Hearing this from a friend, Okonjoro thought this meant there was something wrong with his vision so she ordered the eye medicine. Okonjoro was a smart Bakegitsune, but she could get a little confused.

Data File

⚲ Kasaichi, Higashi, Hamamatsu, Shizuoka prefecture

❀ Beginning Showa period?

📖 *Culture and Climate of Our Kasaichi Town*

🖊 *Konkasuri* is a woven fabric of faint white and dark blue. It can come in various patterns.

Surprising!
Nothing but a careless Kitsune!

Ganbari Nyudo

A floating head that transforms into a gold coin!

Ganbari Nyudo is a Yokai that hides in toilets. Toriyama Sekien illustrated Ganbari Nyudo in his book *Konjyaku Gazu Zoku Hyakki* as the spirt of a priest stretching up from the collection box to peer in the window. However, he's not a Peeping Tom. In fact, he is a guardian who keeps evil creatures from taking up residence in your toilet. On New Year's Eve, if you stand outside your bathroom and say "Ganbari Nyudo hototogisu" (Ganbari Nyudo cuckoo) you will be protected from toilet-dwelling Yokai during the coming year.

Data File

⚥ Throughout Japan?

✳ Edo period?

📖 *Dictionary of Edo Period Literature and Folklore*

✐ Old toilets collected nightsoil for fertilizer. There was a tank under the hole for collecting excrement.

Now that would hardly make our list of strange Yokai if that was all there is to the story. In Matsura Seizan's book *Kashi Yawa* (*Night Stories of the Wood Rat*) there is a legend that says that if you stand by your toilet on New Year's Eve and say the Ganbari Nyudo's name, its head will appear. If you catch the head with the sleeve of your kimono, it will turn into a gold coin.

I'm unsure if Ganbari Nyudo should make us scared or thankful!

Surprising!
A gross guardian spirit from the toilet!

Kyumo Tanuki

An arsonist Bakedanuki?

Kyumo is an unusual name for a Tanuki. He was born in China and slipped aboard a European trading vessel to make his way to Japan. After visiting the shrines, Kyumo settled down with a lovely Mujina (Mujina are generally badgers but also another name for Tanuki in some regions). However, while on their honeymoon a dog attacked and killed his wife. Mad with grief and rage, Kyumo set fire to the town until his anger was spent.

Eventually, Kyumo took up residence in an abandoned mine in Uedanishi, Kibichuo in Okayama prefecture. He adopted a human form and went to the town to help with the rice planting.

When Kyumo shapeshifted, his human body was too short from the waist down, and his beard couldn't hide his pointed face so his disguise was discovered immediately. However, since he wasn't causing any harm and people were afraid he would start fires again if upset, the villagers pretended not to notice.

After that, Kyumo used his mysterious powers to protect the village livestock. He also predicted thefts and fires so they could be prevented. Eventually, the villagers enshrined Kyumo as a local deity. Even so, setting fire to the town seems a bit extreme.

Data File

⚲ Kibichuo, Kagagun, Okayama prefecture

✳ Muromachi – Edo period

📖 *Collection of Kibi*, Vol. 2

🖊 Kyumo Tanuki is enshrined in Karai shrine in Uedanishi, Kibichuo. He is also locally called Maho-sama.

Surprising!
He set the town on fire in revenge!

Konage Baba

A Yokai that attacks by throwing a baby!

Konage Baba appears in the Edo period book *Sanshu Kidan* (*Strange Stories of Three Provinces*). A Samurai named Furuichi Iori kept a manor in a castle town in the Toyama domain. Once, a retainer named Shinzo left on an errand and met an old woman on the way.

Surprising!
A Mujina passing itself
off as another Yokai!

The old woman was holding a baby and without warning, she threw the infant at the retainer. However, Shinzo was prepared. He had heard rumors of a Yokai that would throw a transformed stone that looked like a baby at strangers. Shinzo caught the baby while simultaneously drawing his sword and slashed at the old woman. She let out a scream and vanished.

The next day the retainer followed a trail of blood which led to a hole near the bamboo fence surrounding the manor. Inside was the body of an aged Mujina. The baby-throwing old lady had in fact been a Yokai.

The *Sanshu Kidan* does not name this Yokai. The name Konage Baba first appears in *Yokai Paradaisu* (*Yokai Paradise*). The book's author, Shirakawa Marina, gave it this name.

Data File

⚲ Toyama, Toyama prefecture

☀ Edo period

📖 *Yokai Paradaisu*

🖌 In *Sanshu Kidan*, author Hori Bakusui collected mysterious tales from Kaga (Ishikawa prefecture), Noto (Ishikawa prefecture), and Echu (Toyama prefecture).

Zashiki Warashi

Surprising!
Creepy children that haunt houses!

Legendary gods of fortune.

Zashiki Warashi are Yokai in the Tohoku region that haunt houses in the form of small children. They can appear to be any age from babies to about fifteen years old. Usually, they are invisible and only show themselves when they leave a house.

People who live in houses with Zashiki Warashi talk of hearing small footsteps and children's voices in empty rooms. They are also accompanied by bouts of sleep paralysis. In Tono in Iwate prefecture, it's said that houses with Zashiki Warashi are blessed with good fortune. Alternately, if the spirits leave the house the family will fall into financial ruin and disease.

Data File

⚲ Central to Iwate prefecture in Tohoku region   ❇ Ancient to present

📖 *Zashiki warashi* and *Oshira-sama of Tono*

✍ Warashi can be named according to where they are seen. In the storehouse, they are Storehouse Warashi. Those on the second floor are Second Floor Warashi. Only those in *tatami* rooms called *zashiki* are called Zashiki Warashi.

Because of this, Zashiki Warashi are sometimes seen as gods of fortune. There are also distinct kinds of Zashiki Warashi. For example, in a house in Esashiinase, Oshu, Iwate prefecture, there is a Zashiki Warashi called Itabariko. It crawls around on the dirt floor in the middle of the night but doesn't bring any good luck. It's one of the creepier kinds of Zashiki Warashi.

Daidarabotchi

Surprising!
Giants who created mountains and lakes!

Do giants come in smaller sizes?

Daidarabotchi are large enough for their heads to touch the clouds. There is not just one, but an entire tribe. Legends differ by region but they are usually depicted as giants who build mountains and lakes.

In Shiga prefecture, legends say Mt. Fuji and Lake Biwa were made by Daidarabotchi. Other stories say Daidarabotchi walking across the country made Japan's lakes and marshes. Lake Senba in Ibaraki prefecture, Lake Ashino in Kanagawa prefecture, and Lake Daizahoshi in Nagano prefecture are all said to have been made by rain filling in Daidarabotchi footprints. Looking at the size of these lakes gives a sense of scale for how large Daidarabotchi are.

But along with those giants there are some shrimpy Daidarabotchi as well. A reported footprint on Mt. Ishimaki in Toyohashi, Aichi prefecture, is just over three feet (one meter) in length. That would make this "giant" no more than 33 feet (ten meters) tall. That may sound tall but compared to the mountains that Daidarabotchi are said to create, it's very short.

Data File

⚲ Central to the Kanto region   ☀ Ancient times

📖 *Supplemented Local Legends of Aichi Prefecture*

✒ Daidarabotchi are known by several regional names such as Dandarabotchi, Daidaibo, and Reirabotchi. Some have the characteristics of plague gods called Yakubyogami.

Hitotsume Kozo

A part-time plague god!

Just as the name says, a Hitotsume Kozo (one-eyed boy) is a Yokai boy with one eye. Normally, these mischief-makers are content shocking humans with their single eye. However, in the Izu region of Shizuoka prefecture the story is a little different. Instead of surprising them, they make people sick.

There is a type of Yokai called Yakubyogami, meaning plague gods, who spread disease. Hitotsume Kozo are not normally a Yakubyogami, but for some reason on February 8 and December 8 they join their team. On December 8, the Hitotsume Kozo peek in windows of houses and decide who will get sick. They mark names down in a book.

Data File

⚲ Throughout Japan

❋ Ancient to present

▰ *Kotoyoka – The 8th*

✐ Every town and village has a local guardian deity called Dosojin. They are celebrated at *dondoyaki* festivals where people burn New Year's decorations and protective amulets from the previous year.

Surprising!
It's powerless without its book!

When the book is full, they give it to the local Dosojin guardian deity. The following year they come back on February 8 and retrieve their book from the Dosojin. Everyone whose name is in the book falls ill.

On January 15, towns hold a *dondoyaki* festival where they ritually burn items from the previous year. Some people throw effigies of the Dosojin into the fire, hoping that the flames will burn Hitotsume Kozo's book. This way when Hitotsume Kozo returns on February 8, there is no list of names. With no one to make sick they go back home.

Mujina no Tsuki

Surprising!
A Yokai that rolls itself into a ball!

Mujina that transform into a glowing moon!

Mujina no Tsuki means "Mujina's Moon" and refers to a false moon shining in the sky. A legend from Ibaraki prefecture says Mujina no Tsuki often appear on summer nights, usually floating above a tree. They look as large as the real moon and glow brightly. Then they suddenly disappear from the sky. These false moons are Mujina with amazing shapeshifting abilities. In Yoshi, Chiba prefecture, an ancient legend tells of an old woman sitting on her porch admiring the full moon. "What a beautiful moon," she says. A nearby Mujina hears her and decides to give her a surprise.

Data File

⚲ Throughout Japan

☀ Ancient to present

📖 *Folktales of Choshi*

🖌 Mujina are generally thought to be badgers, but in the Kanto region Mujina can equally refer to Tanuki.

The creature climbs a large tree in the garden and transforms into the moon. The old woman says "Another moon! Although it is awfully low in the sky...." The old woman is not nearly shocked enough for the Mujina, who then rises higher and higher. "A little more," says the old woman. Trying to impress her, the Mujina goes even higher until it runs out of tree and plummets to the ground. While trying to prank the old woman the Mujina got pranked instead!

Yarena Baba

A Bakegitsune who only wanted to ride a horse!

The era of this tale is lost to time, but it tells of a person from Agu, Hikawara, Izumo, Shimane prefecture. This person lived upriver in Hikawara and worked as a porter using a horse to transport goods. Coming home every night he would pass an odd old woman annoyingly shouting "Yarena Yarena! (Dear me!)" One night she pleaded to be let up on the horse, saying "Walking's tough at my age. Let me get a ride!" The porter agreed.

Surprising!

A Kitsune outfoxed by a human!

Data File

◊ Hikawa, Izumo, Shimane prefecture   ☀ Meiji or Showa period?

▣ *Folktales and Songs of Hikawa, Izumo*

∥ "Yarena" is Izumo dialect for "yareyare," meaning "good grief!" or "dear me!"

When the old woman happily climbed on the horse, the porter swiftly threw ropes over her and tied her up. He had long known she was a Kitsune in disguise and thought this was finally his chance to get rid of her. Showing her true form, the Kitsune cried and promised never to do it again. The porter didn't intend her any harm and untied her. He never saw the old woman again.

Called the Yarena Baba, this old Kitsune was not much of a Yokai, being easily fooled by a human.

Tono no Naki Ishi

A stone that cried until it got its way!

In Tono, Iwate prefecture, there are stone monoliths called Continuous Stones. Large rocks are balanced on other large rocks in a mysterious post-and-lintel formation. According to legend, famed warrior Mukashibo Benkei stacked them as he was wandering through the forest. When he finished, the bottom stone complained, "I am a much higher-ranking stone, yet I am on the bottom?" It cried all through the night, and Benkei had no choice but to put that stone on top. It ceased its crying, now towering over the other stones.

Surprising!
A rock that is so sad it cries!

Data File

- ⚲ Ayaori, Tono, Iwate prefecture
- ❋ Heian period?
- 📖 *Tono Mongatari*
- 🖋 Mukashibo Benkei is a legendary warrior monk of the Heian period, who served Minamoto Yoshitsune.

Odori Bozu

A mysterious dancing Yokai!

Mt. Kumanosan in Wakayama prefecture has long been a place of special worship with many pilgrimage routes running throgh the area. One pilgrimage, called Nakahechi, has a difficult trail over Iwagami Pass. It's said that if you sing while going over this pass, a monk will suddenly appear and start dancing along.

Called the Odori Bozu, or Dancing Monk, there is nothing more known about it. Why does it dance? Is its dance harmful to people? We don't know a thing. But the lack of answers makes it all the more mysterious.

Surprising!
No one knows why it dances!

Data File

📍 Hongu, Tanabe, Wakayama prefecture　　🌼 Meiji or Showa period?

📖 *Researching Wakayama*, Volume 5, Dialects and Folklore Studies

🖊 Mt. Kumanosan is home to three important shrines, Kumano Hongu Grand Shrine, Kumano Hayatama Grand Shrine, and Kumano Nachi Grand Shrine. The route linking them is known as the Kumano Pilgrimage.

Sekito Migaki

Cleaning graves of people he doesn't know!

Rumors of the Sekito Migaki started the tenth year of Bunsei (1827), centered around the Kanto region. It is said no one has ever seen a Sekito Migaki, but it appears at night and polishes graves and stone monuments until they glisten. It causes no harm and seems like an incredibly helpful Yokai except that in its vigor to clean it often topples headstones. In truth it is a nuisance.

Some say Sekito Migaki is just kids out causing trouble. Others say it somehow magically cures illnesses. Whatever the truth is, it remains a mystery.

Surprising!
A Yokai that cleans stranger's graves!

Data File

📍 Kanto region ☀ Edo period 📖 *Edo Talk of Fujioka*

✍ There are more than three hundred graves and monuments for the Sekito Migaki to clean in the temples in the Edo neighborhoods of Asakusa and Shitaya alone.

Chichin Tanuki

Data File

◊ Tokushima, Tokushima prefecture

※ Beginning Showa period?

▥ *Tanuki Tales of Awa*

▥ Mt. Bizan is a symbol of Tokushima. It is known for ropeways and roads maintained for sightseers.

Surprising!
A Yokai that acts like an alarm clock!

A Tanuki that won't let people sleep.

Chichin Tanuki is a legend passed down in Tokushima prefecture and is a kind of Mamedanuki. The eastern side of Mt. Bizan is lined with temples and shrines. The Chichin Tanuki played tricks on workers building those holy sites. Workers on the sites often took naps during their breaks. That's when the Chichin Tanuki snuck out and examined their faces. If it found anyone only pretending to be asleep, it said "Chichin! Wake up! Chichin! Open your eyes!"

Why it does this, no one knows. It's a harmless bit of mischief from a cute Tanuki Yokai.

Nando Baba

An ugly old woman that scares children!

Nando means a storage room or bedroom, usually a darker room, preferably without windows. In Miya, Akaiwa, Okayama prefecture, the Nando Baba is said to live in these nando rooms. Looking like a balding old woman, the Nando Baba jumps out and says "Boo!" at anyone who opens the door. But that's all she does. Moreover, if you threaten her with a broom she flees. Nando Baba is a Yokai that only frightens children.

Surprising!
A Yokai that runs away from brooms!

Data File

🜨 Miya, Akaiwa, Okayama prefecture

❀ Beginning Showa period?

📕 *Encyclopedia of Okayama Yokai*

✏ Nando Baba appears in other parts of Japan. In Tobu, Kagawa prefecture, the Nando Baba is said to kidnap children.

Yakan Korogashi

Who is afraid of a rolling pot?

Walking down a hill at night, you hear the unmistakable sound of a pot rolling after you. "Klang Karang!" But when you jump aside to dodge the pot, there is nothing there. That is the Yakan Korogashi. It doesn't actually hurt anyone, just surprises them.

Yakan Korogashi are found all over Japan, although there is disagreement of what they are. They are often portrayed as weasels or Kitsune playing pranks. In any case, most agree the Yokai is not the kettle itself but whatever threw the kettle. Why exactly did they choose a kettle to roll downhill? No one knows. The ways of Yokai are mysterious.

Data File

- ⚲ Throughout Japan
- ❋ Edo period to present
- 📖 *Collection of Japanese Supernatural Tales, Yokai Edition*, Vol. 1
- ✎ Yakan Korogashi are known by different names across Japan, such as Kansu Korobashi in Kashiyama prefecture or Yakan Makuri in Nagano prefecture. But whatever they are called the idea is the same.

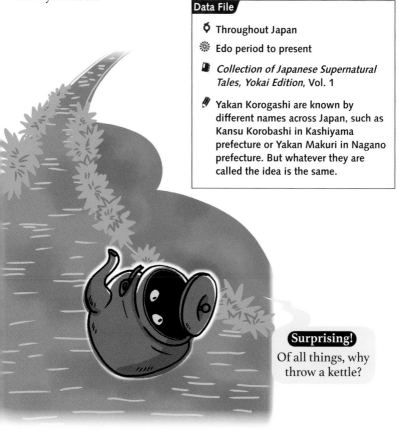

Surprising!
Of all things, why throw a kettle?

Myths and Urban Legends

Myths can be specific to a certain time and place. They often explain how an impressive rock at a Shinto shrine came to be or they might tell of how a partcular set of stone stairs were carved by Oni. Even when clearly fictional, these tales become part of the oral history of the land.

Urban legends are more like neighborhood gossip; they are very often treated as actual events, such as revealing how some local eccentric was actually a Kitsune. Both myths and urban legends are told as fact, and so they can feel real.

Yokai might appear and act differently depending on if the story is a myth or an urban legend.

There are many Yokai that are nasty, naughty or downright disgusting. Whether they do it for fun or because they like to gross out humans, these Yokai are truly rude.

CHAPTER

Disgusting Yokai

Oburoshiki

Special crotch attack!

In the Kotonami district of Manno in Kagawa prefecture, many people made their living burning wood for charcoal in the mountains. They would typically sleep every day in mountain cabins. When spending the night alone in these cabins, woodsmen would sometimes be visited by a strange man. This mysterious visitor was actually the Yokai called Oburoshiki.

At first, he seems polite, sitting cross-legged by the fire. Eventually he reaches under his kimono and pulls out his testicles, warming them. As they heat up, they enlarge and spread out until they look like a giant wrapping cloth called a *furoshiki*.

When large enough, the Oburoshiki launches its special attack, wrapping a victim up in its testicle sack. In most tales, the woodsman throws a burning stick of wood or some charcoal into the Oburoshiki's sack, causing it to flee in agony.

Data File

⚲ Kotonami, Nakatado, Manno, Kagawa prefecture.

❄ Beginning Showa period?

📖 *Stories of Kotonami*

✐ In Kotonami, there are also stories of snakes and baboons that transform and use their testicles to ensnare humans.

Surprising!
Testicles used as a weapon!

There is a similar Yokai called the Kintama Hiroge in the Ikedachi district of Miyoshi, Tokushima prefecture. In both cases the true form of the Yokai is never revealed. However, from its testicular power it is widely assumed to be a Tanuki .

Kaki Otoko

A gross way to eat a persimmon!

Kaki Otoko, meaning "persimmon man," is a Yokai in Mukashi Banashi fairy tales from the Tohoku region. They are the spirits of persimmon trees, appearing before humans as huge men with red faces.

They manifest in households with neglected persimmon trees, laden with unpicked fruit. In one house a Kaki Otoko appeared before a woman who wanted to eat the fruit but couldn't because she was only a household maid.

The Kaki Otoko came to her room at night and handed her a skewer. He told her "Use that to pick something from my butt." Disgusted and about to faint, the maid did as she was told. The Kaki Otoko told her to lick the skewer, and then disappeared.

Normally she wouldn't do such a thing, magic spirit or not, but such a sweet aroma came from the skewer that she gave it a tentative lick. She was amazed at how it tasted like a delicious persimmon.

A magical spirit who comes to a woman who wants to eat persimmons and grants her wish by making her eat from its butt... that certainly is a disgusting Yokai!

Data File

⚲ Tohoku region

❉ Pre-Showa period?

📖 *Kikimimi Zoshi*

✎ Kaki Otoko is called Tantan Kororin in Miyagi prefecture.

Shitagara Gonboku

A Yokai that can't keep its hands to itself!

There's a bridge called Yabashi over the Shiratori River in Ninohe, Iwate prefecture. Around the beginning of the Edo period, there were tales of a Yokai called Shitagara Gonboku that appeared near that bridge.

One night, a Samurai named Yosaburo hid near the bridge planning to ambush and kill the Yokai said to be haunting this area. Waiting for it to appear, he suddenly had to go pee. He couldn't hold it, so he turned towards the river. Without warning, a hand reached up from the darkness and started to grope him.

Startled, Yosaburo drew his sword and cut off the offending hand in a single stroke. Something screamed and ran away.

Data File

♀ Fukuoka Iwayabashi, Ninohe, Iwate prefecture

✺ Edo period

📖 *Legends of Iwate*

⚕ The story of a Tanuki teaching medicine in exchange for a severed hand comes from the Edo period book *Tonoigusa*.

Surprising!
A yokai with absolutely no shame!

That night, a one-handed Tanuki appeared at Yosaburo's house disguised as an old woman. She said, "If you return my hand, I'll teach you how to make an elixir that treats cuts and wounds." Yosaburo gave her back her hand. He became rich making and selling the elixir.

The perverted Yokai in this story is called the Shitagara Gonboku. The name means roughly "That jerk from Shimogawara."

Sukabe

Surprising!
Its name means "silent but deadly!"

Prophecy of toxic fumes!

The Covid pandemic saw a resurgence in popularity of the Edo-period Yokai Amabie. Appearing in broadside *kawaraban*, Amabie prophesized a period of pandemic and disaster.

Sukabe is another of these prophetic creatures. Just like Amabie, it also appeared in *kawaraban*. It said in the mountains of Toyama prefecture, she appeared "From the Imaki Valley Crack in Mt. Kaki in Etchu." It said to those present, "four or five years from now, a disease shall ravage the land, causing farting so powerful your hands will clench and sweat."

However, if you shared the Sukabe's image, the crisis could be averted. There is no record in Japan of a plague of farting, so it must have been successful.

In truth, Sukabe is a parody of Yokai like Kutahe (found on page 186). Even the location where it was found, Imaki Valley Crack, is a joke.

Data File

⚲ Toyama prefecture?

✳ Edo period?

📖 *Discoveries of the Mysteries of Mt. Tate?!*

✎ Kawaraban were Edo period newspapers. They were printed using the wood-block printing method.

Pawci

Witches who love to dance naked!

Pawci are naughty witches from the Ainu people of northern Japan. They live on the banks of the Susurampet River in High Heaven, where they dance naked in joy with a group of equally naked men.

Data File

⚲ Hokkaido

☀ Ancient to present?

📖 *Collection of Ainu Folk Traditions*

✍ In the Sonkyo mountain gorges of Kamikawa, Hokkaido, there are collections of massive rock formations that form a ravine. Popular with tourists, these formations are said to be a Pawci fortress.

Occasionally, they come down to earth to seduce humans and enlarge their dancing circle of madness. The Pawci dance encircles the entire globe.

Pawci also have the ability to possess people. Those who are said to be possessed by Pawci become lecherous and adulterous. Many a cheating spouse claimed their immoral behavior was caused by temporary Pawci possession.

Pawci are Kamui, meaning "gods" in Ainu traditions. They live in High Heaven and are deities of kimono making. However, they are not good at heart. Their mischievous nature lures them away from heaven and into causing trouble in the typical Yokai way.

Surprising!
Freaky Yokai who dance in the nude!

Ringo no Sei

The Kaki Otoko's gross brother!

A Mukashi Banashi tells a tale from the Kakunodate region of Akita prefecture of one of the grossest Yokai ever, the Ringo no Sei, meaning "apple spirit."

Once, an old man lived alone in a village. One evening, a mysterious man visited. Without warning, the stranger suddenly said, "I would love to eat some poop." The old man was confused but wanted to be a good host. He pooped on a plate and served it to his guest. The stranger happily dug in, exclaiming "Oooh! This is so delicious!"

The stranger then made his own poop and offered it up for the the old man to try. Curious, he took a tentative bite. It was more delicious than he could have ever imagined. After that, the stranger returned every night, and they took turns eating each other's poop.

Eventually, the old man became disturbed by this. The next time the stranger came by, he pulled out a hatchet and struck him, chasing him out of his house.

In the morning, he followed the stranger's footsteps. They led to an ancient apple tree, which had a deep cut from a hatchet. The old man realized his visitor had been the spirit of this apple tree, and his poop had been the fruit of this tree. In return, the tree wanted the old man's poop for fertilizer.

Surprising!

An old man eating apple poop!

Data File

⚥ Akita prefecture

❀ Beginning Showa period?

📖 *Travel and Legends*, Vol. 13, No. 5

✎ It's not known if the apples and trees are from Meiji-period cultivated Western apples or wild Japanese apples.

Okkeruipe

Surprising!
An invisible Yokai
with farts you can
hear and smell!

Data File

- ♀ Karafuto region (Modern day Sakhalin Oblast, Russia)

- ※ Beginning Showa period?

- 📖 *Collection of Ainu Folk Traditions*

- 🖊 Okkeruipe is also known as Okke Oyaji. Both mean something like "flatulence monster."

An invisible fart monster!

Okkeruipe comes from Ainu legends from the Karafuto region that used to be part of Japan but is today part of Russia. The story tells of a person living alone, who suddenly hears a fart from the fireplace along with a terrible stench. Farts then start exploding from every corner of the room. The smell gets so bad the person runs from the house.

There is an easy way fight back. If you answer the first fart with a fart of your own, or even make a fart noise with your mouth, the okkeruipe will flee. It is otherwise a harmless, yet stinky, Yokai.

Kainade

The shameless Yokai of Setsubun!

Tales of Yokai called Kainade come from Kyoto, during a time when drop toilets were in common use. For unexplained reasons they only appeared on the night of Setsubun, a festival celebrating the beginning of Spring. When anyone sat on the toilet, the Kainade would raise up a hairy hand and stroke their bottom.

Anyone using the toilet on Setsubun night could ward off the Kainade by saying a simple spell, asking "Should I use red paper or white paper?" If that was said, the Kainade would keep its hands to itself.

Why did it touch people's butts? Why on Setsubun night? Honestly, nothing about this Yokai makes sense.

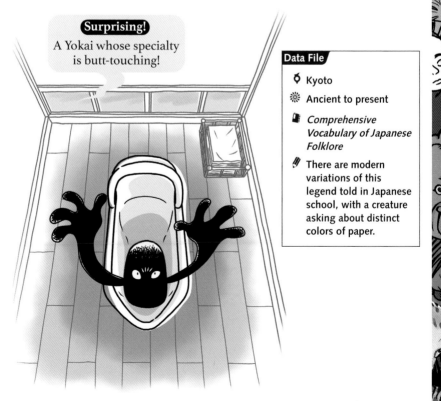

Surprising!
A Yokai whose specialty is butt-touching!

Data File

- ⚲ Kyoto
- ☀ Ancient to present
- 📘 *Comprehensive Vocabulary of Japanese Folklore*
- ✎ There are modern variations of this legend told in Japanese school, with a creature asking about distinct colors of paper.

Karasade Baba

Don't go to the bathroom on November 26!

Kainade appears on Setsubun, but in the Izumo region a Yokai called Karasade Baba comes out of the toilet on November 26 of the lunar calendar. Even worse, instead of the gentle furry touch of the Kainade, the Karasade Baba claws your butt.

On that day, both adults and children make sure they go to the bathroom before night falls.

Also, in Matsue, around Furue, it's an old man, not an old woman who hides in the toilet. But man or woman, this is one naughty Yokai!

Data File

🜨 Izumo, Shimane prefecture   ☀ Ancient to present

📖 *Folklore*, Vol. 14, No. 5

✎ Before the Meiji period, Japan used a lunar calendar based on the phases of the Moon and the movement of the Sun.

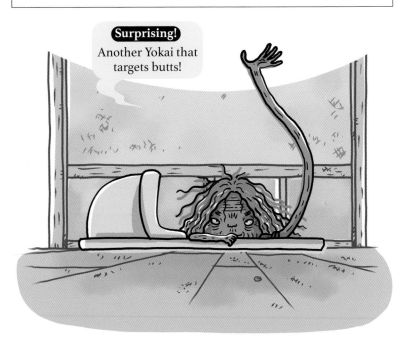

Surprising!
Another Yokai that targets butts!

Sagaimata

Right in the crotch!

Written with the characters meaning "hanging crotch," this yokai lives up to its name. It appears as the bottom half of a human hanging from a big tree. Sagaimata appear on roads with steep sides or slopes where trees and shrubbery form a tunnel. Passing through such lonely paths in the dark, you might run into a tree with a pair of legs and a crotch dangling down.

Careless travelers will find themselves scissored by these dangling legs. They are then dragged up into the tree and eaten. The fact that they are eaten means there must be a mouth somewhere in that crotch.

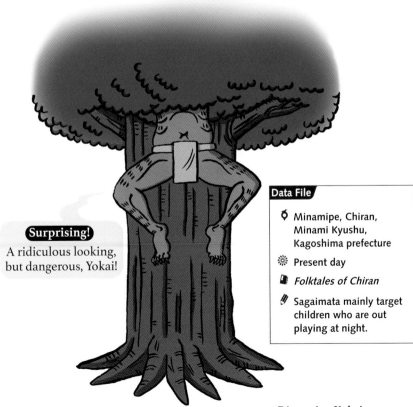

Surprising!

A ridiculous looking, but dangerous, Yokai!

Data File

⚲ Minamipe, Chiran, Minami Kyushu, Kagoshima prefecture

☼ Present day

📖 *Folktales of Chiran*

✎ Sagaimata mainly target children who are out playing at night.

Shoben Nomi

A taste for people's pee!

In Kotonami ward of Manno in Kagawa prefecture, there's a Yokai that loves human urine. There are many in that area who make their living burning charcoal in the mountains. They sleep in the mountain cabins and when they have to pee in the middle of the night, they go in a tub outside. When they wake up the next morning, the tub is dry.

Something came out in the night and drank every drop. No one knows what a Shoben Nomi looks like as they have never been seen. They aren't dangerous at all, just gross.

Surprising!
A Yokai that gulps down human urine!

Data File

📍 Kotonami, Manno, Kagawa prefecture   ☀ Ancient to present

📖 *Stories of Kotonami*

✍ The true nature of the Shoben Nomi is likely the now-extinct Japanese wolf or some other form of wildlife. Animals in the wild often drink human urine.

What do you do if you meet a Yokai? In the olden days people thought about how to fight back.
Yokai also have weaknesses.

CHAPTER

4

Yokai Countermeasures and Weaknesses

Ubume

Watch out for the murderous baby!

It's said that a woman who dies in childbirth and is unable to find peace might linger in the living world as an Ubume. They often appear on riversides and crossroads, asking passersby if they would please hold their baby for just a moment.

Good samaritans who hold the baby find it growing heavier. Ultimately the passersby are killed, either by being crushed or having their throats torn out by the baby.

Your best bet is to run away immediately. But if you have already taken the baby, there are a few things you can do.

In the Shimabara area of Nagasaki prefecture, a simple way to defeat the Ubume has been passed down. When you take the baby, keep it facing away from you so it can't bite you, and sit with your butt on the ground so it can get as heavy as it wants without crushing you.

If you succeed, the Ubume will grant you some sort of reward, either in the form of treasure or a bestowing of supernatural powers. As to why Ubume want people to hold their babies, no one knows.

Data File

◊ Throughout Japan ☀ Ancient to present

📖 *Japanese Kaidan Collection Yurei Edition*

✎ In Akita prefecture, it's said Ubume can grant powers through a technique called *obojikara*. Those endowed with this power have four legs and arms.

Surprising!
An evil Yokai that is easy to defeat!

Umibozu

Surprising!
A Yokai that runs away when it's told it's not scary!

Defeated by the power of the human spirit?

Umibozu are Yokai who appear at sea or near the beach. They have big, round heads, and look similar to a pitch-black version of the Yokai called Onyudo.

Their attacks are brutal, sinking ships and dragging people under the waves. Even catching a glimpse of an Umibozu is said to be an omen of misfortune. They are one of the greatest fears of hunters and sailors. It's said Umibozu appear on stormy days, at the ends of months, and during the festivals of Obon and New Year's Eve.

One day, cargo ship captain Kuwanaya Tokuzo left port alone on New Year's Eve. The weather suddenly turned rough, and a dark shape rose from the waters, towering nearly ten feet (three meters) tall. It asked, "Aren't I frightening?" Defiantly, Tokuzo answered "Not as terrifying as having to earn your way in this world!"

Hearing this, the Umibozu looked dejected and sullenly sunk beneath the waves.

Not all Umibozu are this wimpy, running away as soon as someone stands up to them. This was a particularly pitiful Umibozu.

Data File

⚬ Throughout Japan   ☸ Ancient to present

📖 *Animal Yokai Collection*, Vol. 1

〽 Cargo ships called *kitamaebune* sailed the ports between Osaka and Hokkaido, moving trade goods across Japan. They supported logistics at the time.

Kawauso

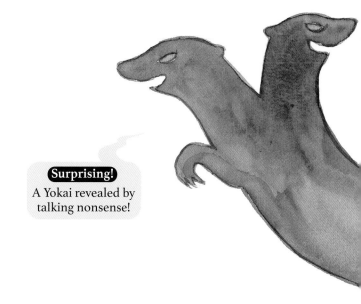

Surprising!
A Yokai revealed by
talking nonsense!

Data File

♦ Throughout Japan

✳ Beginning Showa period?

📖 *New Edition: Yokai Discourse*

✎ There has not been a sighting of Kawauso (Japanese otters) since 1979. In 2012, they were officially declared extinct. However, some researchers have not given up and say there is still the possibility some survive. The search continues.

Strange words give the game away.

Across Japan, river otters, known as Kawauso, mastered the art of shape changing. They use this power to decieve and generally annoy human beings. For example, in Toto peninsula in Ishikawa prefecture, Kawauso masquerade as young women aged about twenty, or as children in checkered kimonos. Thus disguised, they wait by the side of the road for someone to fool.

But there are ways to spot Kawauso pretending to be humans.

All you have to do is ask the Kawauso two simple questions. The first is "Where are you?" A human will say, "Huh? I'm right here." But a Kawauso will say "I'm over there." When you ask them, "Where do you live?" for some reason they always answer "Kahai." By their nonsensical answers you will know they are not humans and mostly likely Kawauso.

Kawauso are dangerous and their mischief often results in death or injury for their victims, usually by biting. However, if you know what they are, you should be able to get away without falling into their trap.

Sarakazoe

Adding one did the trick?

Sarakazoe, or plate-counting Yurei (ghost), appears in the Saraya-shiki legend. The story has been told across Japan since ancient times, from the northern Tohoku region to the southern island of Kyushu. It has been been performed in classical Japanese theater both as *Banshu Sarayashiki* and *Bancho Sarayashiki*.

Data File

○ Throughout Japan   ❀ Pre-Edo period?   ▦ *Legends of Japan's Sarayashiki*

▨ In Western Japan, Sarayashiki is performed as the Kabuki play titled *Banshu Sarayashiki* set in Himeji castle. In eastern Japan, it is a Kodan performance called *Bancho Sarayashiki* and is set in the Bancho region of Edo, now modern day Chiyoda.

Surprising!
A Yurei that is banished through trickery!

The title tells you what the story is all about. There was a young woman who worked at a *yashiki*, or grand mansion. Her name is often given as Okiku. The lord of the manor had a set of ten valuable plates, or *sara*. One of them was broken, and in anger the lord blamed and killed Okiku.

That night, Okiku's spirit appeared, and counted the plates one-by-one. When she got to nine, she cried in sorrow, unable to find the missing plate.

A version of *Bancho Sarayashiki* told in Matsue, Shimane prefecture, boarders on comedy. The lord asks a virtuous Buddhist monk for help. The monk hides in a bush and waits for Okiku. When she counted to nine, he shouted ten. Hearing that, the Sarakazoe never appeared again.

Zarazara Zattara

Watch out for rolling pumpkins!

Zarazara Zattara, also known as Zazara Zattara, are Yokai that appear in a Mukashi Banashi tale from Shizuoka prefecture. They look like a pumpkin and move by rolling around.

They're usually found in the mountains. They look for cabins with only one occupant then roll into them. When the person notices something strange, a voice in their head says "Don't worry. It's only a Zarazara Zattara. Nothing to worry about." And when they think they should get out of the cabin, the voice says "No no. It will be gone soon. Everything's fine."

Surprising!
A Yokai unable to avoid
sudden attacks!

This is most likely a type of Yokai called a Satori. They have the ability to read people's minds. And like with Satori, the only way to get rid of them is with a sudden, unexpected attack.

In one case of a Zarazara Zattara attack, a mountain man tossed a stick on the fire in his cabin, part of which broke off and hit the Yokai in the face. Taken by surprise, the Zarazara Zattara rolled out of the cabin in fear.

The ability to read minds is dangerous, but it doesn't give the ability to predict sudden actions.

Data File

⚲ Shizuoka prefecture　　☀ Beginning Showa period?

📖 *Collection of Legends and Mukashi Banashi of Shizuoka Prefecture*

✎ Satori are also called Mind Monsters. They visit mountain cabins at night and read the minds of those within.

Shigama Nyobo

Surprising!
A Yokai with a body that melts!

Spirits of icicles hanging from houses.

Shigama is another word for icicle. Shigama Nyobo are also known as Tsurara Onna, or icicle woman. They are found in Mukashi Banashi stories from the frozen north of Japan. This story comes from the Tsugaru region of Aomori prefecture.

One winter morning, a man who lived alone saw the icicles hanging from the eaves of his house. He muttered, "I wish I knew a woman as slender and beautiful as that."

That night, a woman knocked on his door. She was slender and beautiful, and as she stepped in his house she said, "I've come to be your bride." They fell instantly in love and were soon happily married. The only thing that annoyed him was that his wife never took a bath.

One night, after forcing her into a hot bath, she disappeared. All that was left was the comb she wore in her hair, floating in the water.

The tale of the Shigama Nyobo is a sad one. Of course, for one whose body is made of ice, they melt when forced into hot water. But even if she hadn't gone into the bath, she would have melted when spring came. Their parting was only a question of time.

Data File

⚲ Tohoku and Northern Japan

✹ Beginning Showa period?

📖 *Japanese Kaidan Collection, Yokai Edition*, Vol. 2

🗡 Shigama Nyobo are most commonly spirits of icicles. In some Mukashi Banashi, they are not icicles but are children of Yuki Onna.

Seko

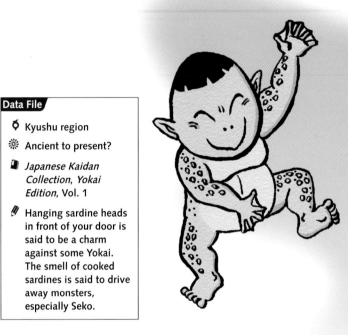

Data File

- ⚲ Kyushu region
- ※ Ancient to present?
- 📖 *Japanese Kaidan Collection, Yokai Edition*, Vol. 1
- ✍ Hanging sardine heads in front of your door is said to be a charm against some Yokai. The smell of cooked sardines is said to drive away monsters, especially Seko.

A Yokai that hates sardine heads!

Seko live in the mountains around Oita, Nagasaki, in Kumamoto and Miyagi prefectures (See page 101). They live in packs, and while they are usually unseen, in their physical form they commonly have a single eye on a childlike body. There are various kinds of Seko with each prefecture describing them differently. For example, the Seko above have two eyes.

It is said that Seko are mischievous Kappa who have taken to the mountains and changed form. In Notsu, Usuki, Oita prefecture, Seko are said to imitate human speech.

Surprising!
If they even hear someone mention sardine heads they run away!

They think it is funny to tug on the hands or feet of women and children.

It's said there are unseen Seko paths through the mountains, and those who sleep in mountain cabins are kept up at night by the noise of Seko building their roads and waystations. When that happens, the mountain men will yell "We've got sardine heads here!" Seko flee at the mere mention of the thing they hate the most.

Why they hate fish if they were formerly Kappa is a mystery.

Funa Yurei

Murderous ghosts that haunt the sea.

There is no creature in Japan's seas more terrifying than Funa Yurei. They are quite different from Yokai who get their kicks pranking humans. Funa Yurei drag people under the waves and drown them.

Funa Yurei look like Yurei, or ghosts, of people who died at sea. They appear on stormy nights when the fog lies thick.

Data File

⚲ Throughout Japan ☀ Ancient to present?

📖 *Japanese Kaidan Collection, Yurei Edition*, Vol. 1

✎ The appearance of Funa Yurei varies according to the era. When Japanese-style boats were common that's what they sailed in. But when motorized boats took over, Funa Yurei started appearing in them.

Surprising!
Yurei who don't notice
if their water ladle
has holes!

Funa Yurei sail in a phantom ship. Their goal is to increase the size of their group by adding new souls. They pull alongside a vessel and demand to be given a water ladle. Every boat has a special bailing ladle called a *hishaku* used to empty water that accumulates on the bottom. That is what they want.

When given the ladle, they use it to pour water from the sea into the boat until it sinks to the bottom. In defense, boats would carry special *hishaku* with holes drilled into the bottom. They would hand these to the Funa Yurei who would then fruitlessly attempt to use them to fill the boat. But of course, the water drained from the *hishaku* and not a drop went into the vessel. Eventually they would give up and disappear.

This sounds silly, but it was the most effective countermeasure against Funa Yurei.

Mikari Baba

A Yokai that steals eyes and baskets.

In Kanagawa prefecture and the Tamachi area of Tokyo tales are told of a Yokai called Mikari Baba that wanders around houses on the evenings of the 8th of February and December. They look for houses with *mi*, a traditional type of winnowing basket used for sifting rice and grains on farms.

It's often said the "mi" in Mikari Baba refers to this basket, but in fact it also refers to eyeballs, or "me" in Japanese. Their name means "eyeball-borrowing old woman." They only have one eye, so it seems they feel the need to snatch another one from humans.

Whether you have *mi* (winnowing baskets) or *me* (eyeballs), your house is in trouble when a Mikari Baba comes around.

To defend against Mikari Baba, bamboo baskets are hung on poles throughout villages on the 8th of February and December. To the one-eyed Mikari Baba, these hanging baskets look like hundreds of eyes. Humans can't really understand why, but one-eyed creatures tend to be terrified of many-eyed creatures, so they flee in fear.

Data File

- ♂ Kanto region
- ※ Ancient to present?
- 📓 *Kotoyoka – The 8th*
- ✎ In some areas Mikari Baba are said to have two eyes while in others they hold a flaming stick in their teeth and fly in the sky.

Surprising!
A dangerous Yokai that is afraid of bamboo baskets!

Mikoshi Nyudo

Whatever you do, don't look up!

The Yokai called Mikoshi Nyudo appear on slopes late at night. At first, they appear as small humans. Then they slowly start to grow larger. As a person watches them grow, they get taller and taller, as tall as the person watching them is able to look up.

If a person looks up so far they fall backwards, the Mikoshi Nyudo stomps on their throat and kills them.

However, Mikoshi Nyudo are easy to defeat. When they stretch, instead of watching them grow, stare down at their feet. They can't actually grow if no one watches them.

There are other defenses as well. In Sadogashima, Nigata prefecture, they are called Miagari Nyudo. When encountering one, if you say, "Look up, Miagari Nyudo!" then stare at the ground, it will disappear.

In Kawanihon, Shizuoka prefecture, there is a legend of a carpenter meeting a Mikoshi Nyudo. Marveling at the growing creature, the carpenter whipped out a T-square to measure its height. It suddenly vanished.

For some reason, Mikoshi Nyudo hate having their height measured.

Data File

- ⚲ Throughout Japan
- ☀ Ancient to present?
- 📖 *Legends and Mukashi Banashi of Shizuoka Prefecture*
- ✎ In the Edo period, another type of Mikoshi Nyudo surprised people by leaning over them from behind.

Surprising!

A giant Yokai who doesn't want its height measured!

Surprising!

Even if they transform, they're still the same jerks!

Yokai Countermeasures and Weaknesses

Yamawaro

Mischievous Yokai from the mountains!

Yamawaro are Yokai that look a little like human children and are found in the mountainous regions of the island of Kyushu. They love to cause mischief for woodcutters by imitating the sound of falling trees or pulling on their horses. On the other hand, with their friendly nature, they can easily be bribed with food to help in tasks like hauling logs.

Interestingly enough, it's said that many Yamawaro are actually Kappa. In autumn, the Kappa leave their rivers and go up into the mountains. While they are in the mountains they change shape

Data File

⚲ Western Japan

❄ Ancient to present?

📖 *Folktale Collection of Kumamoto Prefecture*

✎ Yamawaro from Kyushu only have one eye. They're known by different names, such as Seko, Karikobo, Young Folk of the Mountains, and Warodon.

and live together in tribes. When spring arrives, they come down from the mountains and return to the rivers as Kappa.

No matter which forms they take, their likes and dislikes remain the same. For example, Kappa hate metal farm implements. In Yatsushiro, Kumamoto prefecture, there's a story told of a Yamawaro who approached a mountain hut one night to do some mischief but found a saw leaning across the entrance. The sight of the saw frightened the Yamawaro so much that it fled into the night.

Nobody really knows why Kappa transform into Yamawaro but the belief is that there is a connection between the deities of the mountains and rivers.

Surprising!
Giant Yokai that shrink with a simple command!

Yuri

A Yokai that transforms into a giant!

Yuri is derived from the word "Yurei," or ghost, and comes from the Yanbara area of northern Okinawa. Yuri appear at Amesoko racetrack (horse races) in the village of Nakajinn. They have long black hair that hides their faces and they wear white kimonos.

Yuri appear suddenly in front of people on night roads, blocking their path and can grow to ridiculous heights. They may grow as tall as the tallest skyscraper with their heads touching the heavens. Like many Yokai, their only intent is to frighten people.

When you meet a Yuri, calmly say "Up, up" and they will grow. Then say "Down, down" and they will shrink back down. If you strike them with a tree branch they will disappear in a flash of light, like a firefly.

If you know how to beat them they are not scary at all.

Data File

⚲ Nakijin, Okinawa prefecture

✳ Around beginning Showa period?

📖 *Local Customs of Yanbara*

✒ The Yuri's gender is not known, but because of the long hair they are thought to be female.

Tatekuri Kaietsu

Surprising!
If you step out of the way, you're in the clear!

Data File

⚲ Hata, Kochi prefecture ※ Ancient to present?

📖 *Japanese Kaidan Collection, Yokai Edition*, Vol. 1

✍ Teginobo is another form of Tatekuri Kaietsu. They take the form of *khakkhara*, monk's staffs topped with iron rings, and jangle while doing somersaults.

A Yokai that flips people on their backs!

Tatekuri Kaietsu is a Yokai that lives in the mountains of Kochi prefecture. They appear as a *tegine*, a type of pestle with a handle in the center that flairs on both ends.

Travelers on mountain roads can hear the sound "stam! stam!" as the Tatekuri Kaietsu somersaults towards them. They speed at flustered people in order to flip them over onto their backs.

That's it. That's all the Tatekuri Kaietsu does. It's just one of many Yokai that likes to prank humans.

If you don't want to get flipped onto your back, then all you have to do is step out of the way. Once they get going, Tatekuri Kaietsu can't change direction. If you step aside, they will go flying past you, unable to stop.

Nunogarami

A killer cloth with a strange weakness!

Menonuma is a large swamp in Takkonagasaka, Takko, in Aomori prefecture. The lord of the swamp is the Nunogarami.

Nunogarami transform to look like strips of cloth that hang from tree branches in the swamp. If anyone is foolish enough to grab the cloths, it is the last thing they will ever do. The Nunogarami stretches out its body, wrapping up its victim and drags them into the swamp to their deaths.

For some strange reason this fearsome Yokai can't stand pigeon eggs. If they get any egg whites on them, Nunogarami fall into the swamp and die.

No one knows the true form of Nunogarami. It is highly possible they are some sort of snake.

Data File

- ♦ Takkonagasaka, Takko, Sannoe, Aomori prefecture
- ❄ Beginning Edo period?
- 📖 *Legends of Aomori*
- ✎ In Kuranuma, Sanoe, there is a story of a snake who rules the local swamp. It transforms into a straw raincoat and hat and positions itself for its victims to wear. When a person wearing this straw raincoat and hat tries to take them off, the snake drags them into the swamp to kill them. It's similar to the Nunogarami.

Surprising!
A Yokai killed by a tiny pigeon egg!

Yokai Origins ❸

Emakimono Yokai

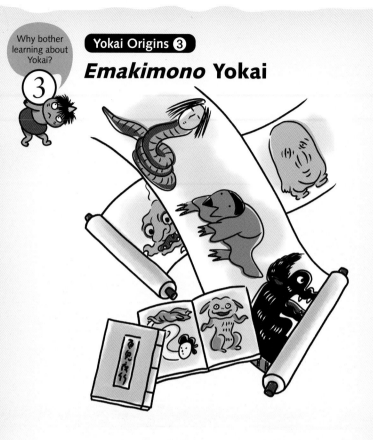

In the Edo period, illustrated books and scrolls featuring Yokai became immensely popular. Artists churned out picture scrolls, called *emakimono*. Popular titles included *Night Parade of 100 Demons* and *Assorted Yokai*. They mixed portrayals of traditional Yokai along with new creatures from their own imaginations.

Emakimono Yokai have amusing bodies and are essentially sight gags. You could think of them as precursors to graffiti. In the Edo period, ukiyo-e artist Toriyama Sekien created Yokai by visualizing common sayings and puns, like Boroboro Ton (page 177) and Yamaoroshi (page 178).

Some Yokai come from folklore and oral storytelling traditions, and some are visual designs from an artist's imagination. It is important to draw a distinction between the two.

The true appearances of Yokai are often different from what you might think. And for some, the way they actually look can be disappointing. Many never existed at all.

CHAPTER

5

Unexpected Origins

Unexpected Origins

Azukitogi Baba

Surprising!

A Yokai that is a Western wooden statue come to life!

Its true origin is not even from Japan!

These Yokai are found by rivers at night. Sometimes known as the Azukitogi (red bean polisher) or the Azukiarai (red bean washer), they are usually heard but not seen. They're mostly identified by the sound of beans being washed, Zakuzaku Shokishoki.

Azukitogi are known across Japan with varied regional differences. In some regions, they're described as looking like old women, where they are called Azuki Baba or Azukitogi Baba. In Kamihanedachi, Sano, Tochigi prefecture, Azukitogi Baba sits by the river and make sounds like "zaaa zaaa!"

Data File

- Kamihanedachi, Sano, Tochigi prefecture
- Beginning Showa period?
- *History of Sano – Folklore Edition*
- Both the Azukitogi Baba and Azuki Arai sing a song that says, "Shall I wash my beans? Or shall I catch someone to eat?"

In the strangest variation, bean-washing sounds are rumored to come from the Kannon-do Hall at Ryukoin temple. Because of this, the Azukitogi Baba was thought to be a statue come to life, specifically the wooden statue called Kateki-sama.

The statue of Kateki-sama was unlike anything else in Japan, with a strange, hooded hat and unusual features. It was discovered during the Taisho period that Kateki-sama was actually a statue of the Christian philosopher Desiderius Erasmus. The statue had been an ornament on a Dutch sailing vessel that washed ashore on Kyushu island before making its way to Ryukoin temple.

A mysterious image from an unknown country? No wonder people thought it was a Yokai.

Karazake no Bakemono

Thousands of fish that combine to make a single Yokai!

Karazake is a type of unsalted, dried salmon. The legend of Karazake no Bakemono comes from Ueno, Ayabe, Kyoto prefecture.

Long ago in Ueno, there was a large lake. A road to the capital city of Kyoto ran alongside the lake. One day, a *karazake* maker was on the road, traveling between Kyoto and the province of Tango. Near the lakeshore, he found a pheasant in a trap. He decided he would make a trade of his *karazake* for the pheasant.

The hunter who set the trap was shocked to say the least at catching *karazake* instead of a tasty pheasant. He threw the cheap, dried fish into the lake.

In the lake, the *karazake* bonded together and came to life. Soon, the monstrous fish became lord of the lake, craving human blood.

A few years later, the *karazake* maker heard the story of this monster and realized it was the angry spirit of the discarded fish he had traded for the pheasant. He thought he should take

Data File

⚲ Fujiyama, Ueno, Ayabe, Kyoto prefecture

✳ Beginning Edo period?

📖 *Legends of Kyoto*

✐ The pestle used to grind the Karazake no Bakemono to powder is enshrined at Wakamiya Shrine in Ueno, in a dedicated Shrine of the Pestle.

responsibility and get rid of the creature. So he traveled back to the lake and when the Karazake no Bakemono appeared, he shouted at it "You're nothing more than cheap fish jerky!"

Exposed and humiliated, the Karazake no Bakemono was unable to maintain its form...some Yokai lose their supernatural abilities when their true forms are revealed. The Karazake no Bakemono collapsed into a pile of dried fish which the maker crushed into a powder with a pestle.

This story shows that given the right circumstances anything can become a Yokai, even a discarded pile of fish jerky.

Surprising!
Exposing its true nature renders it powerless!

Nue

> **Surprising!**
> It's not a real Nue
> but it's called a Nue!

A beast that nearly killed an emperor with its cry!

The most famous story of the Nue comes from the Heian period. It tells of a monster killed by the legendary archer Minamoto no Yorimasa.

Every night that dark clouds gathered above the Imperial palace a strange beastly cry came from the clouds, calling "Hiiiii Hyooooo!" Hearing this mysterious sound, the emperor fell deathly ill. The emperor commanded legendary archer Minamoto no Yorimasa to silence the cries so he took up his bow and with a single shot killed the unseen beast hidden in the clouds.

The body that fell had the face of a monkey, the body of a Tanuki, the legs of a tiger, and a snake for a tail. It was like nothing anyone had ever seen.

Because the beast's cry sounded like that of the Nue bird (the White's thrush) the mysterious creature came to also be called a Nue. Nue means "night crier" which fit the nature of the beast. Because of its lonely call at night, the White's thrush, also known as the "lion's thrush," has long been considered an ominous bird.

As recorded, the yokai Yorimasa shot was called the "beast that cried like a Nue." But that is too long to say so it was soon shortened simply to simply Nue.

Data File

⚥ Kyoto, Kyoto prefecture　　❈ Heian period

📖 *Animal Yokai Collection*, Vol. 1

✎ The corpse of the "beast that cried like a Nue" was placed on a boat and floated down the Kamogawa River. It seemed the curse traveled with it when it drifted ashore.

Abura Bozu

Data File

- Kyoto, Kyoto prefecture
- Heian period
- *Heike Monogatari*
- Taira no Tadamori was a military commander of the Heian period. At Yasaka Shrine, the stone lantern still exists that the Abura Bozu was trying to set on fire. It's called the Tadamori Lantern.

Surprising!
A Yokai that isn't truly a Yokai!

A light that flickers in shrines at night.

This story takes place in the ancient capital of Kyoto. One rainy night the abbot Shiragawa was walking the grounds of Yasaka Shrine, when he saw a suspicious light shining inside. Fearing it was an Oni or some other Yokai come to desecrate the holy shrine, he commanded the warrior Taira no Tadamori to investigate.

Tadamori crept into the shrine. As he neared the light, he was startled to see an elderly monk trying to light the stone lanterns in the falling rain. What the abbot thought was some invading Yokai was no more than the reflection of the light on the old monk's raincoat.

This story is recorded in the book *Heike Monogatari* as the "Tale of the Abura Bozu." It's not really a Yokai, just a trick of the light.

Ubagahi

A mysterious light in the sky.

Long ago, in the vicinity of Hiraoka Shrine in Higashi-osaka, Osaka prefecture, a floating light could occasionally be seen. This was the Yokai Ubagahi, or "hag light."

Legend says there once was an old woman who crept into Hiraoka Shrine each night to steal the oil from the lanterns. When she died, she transformed into a Yokai who continued to haunt the shrine.

Sometimes, when the fire dipped in front of people, if they looked closely, they could see a heron flying in the night sky. From a distance the bird resembled a ball of fire. Sometimes, birds flying at night crackle with static electricity giving them an unearthly glow. Most likely that is the true nature of the Ubagahi.

Surprising!
Probably nothing more than static electricity!

Data File

📍 Izumoichi, Higashi-osaka, Osaka prefecture

❀ Edo period?   📖 *Encyclopedia of the Strange and Mysterious*

✏ In times before electricity, oil was used to light the stone lanterns that provided illumination for shines and other buildings. Shrines and temples used only the finest oil which made them targets for thieves.

Ote no Shiroketsu

A pale butt in the dark!

This story comes from what is now Toyoma, Tome, Miyagi prefecture. Long ago, a Samurai employed at a castle was on his way home. He crossed the bridge over the moat. Suddenly a pale butt appeared under the bridge and started screaming.

The Samurai immediately drew his sword and cut the monster down.

However, it was no monster, just a regular human being. Pulling the corpse from the moat, they saw it was a servant of that same Samurai. Apparently, he was a weirdo who thought it was funny to spook people as they crossed the moat.

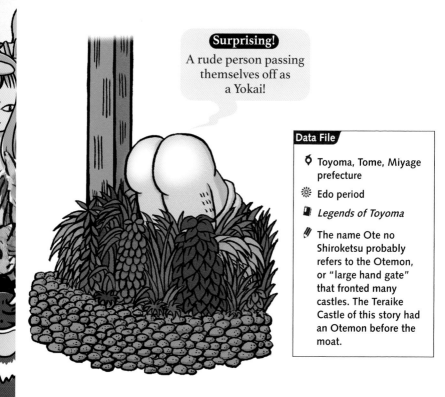

Surprising!
A rude person passing themselves off as a Yokai!

Data File

- Toyoma, Tome, Miyage prefecture
- Edo period
- *Legends of Toyoma*
- The name Ote no Shiroketsu probably refers to the Otemon, or "large hand gate" that fronted many castles. The Teraike Castle of this story had an Otemon before the moat.

Gashadokuro

Surprising!
A legendary Yokai that never truly existed!

Data File

♦ Unknown ※ Unknown

▣ *The Most Detailed Illustrated Japanese Yokai Book*

✎ Gashadokuro comes from an illustration in an Edo period storybook called *Soma no Furudairi, of the Ancient Capital of Soma.* It depicts a scene where princess Takiyasha summons a skeleton by magic.

This yokai is totally made up?

The Gashadokuro is a Yokai that towers hundreds of feet high, made from the bones of the countless dead. It makes the rattling sound "gasha-gasha" as it walks, giving it its name.

Actually, this Yokai was invented in the Showa period, in a children's book. The image was taken from a book by the artist Utagawa Kuniyoshi which depicted an entirely different creature.

Regardless of its modern invention, the Gashadokuro has appeared as a traditional Yokai in multiple comics and animation. It moved quickly from fiction to folklore.

Kamimai

A Yokai or just windblown paper?

Kamimai is a Yokai that scatters stacks of paper in a room as if they were blown by the wind, but there is no wind at all.

In reality, this Yokai does not really exist. It first appeared in a book. The book shows an illustration of tissue paper flying around a room. In fact, this picture comes from a book titled *Record of the Inou Mononoke*, which illustrates a legend from Miyoshi in Hiroshima prefecture.

The picture has nothing to do with a Yokai called Kamimai. The reason for including it as an entry is unknown.

Surprising!
A Yokai created by a mislabled picture!

Data File

♀ Unknown   ✸ Unknown

📖 *Complete Collection of Discourse on Yokai Art*, Vol. 1

✎ In the book *Record of the Inou Mononoke*, an evil demon named Sanmoto Gorozaemon terrorizes a boy named Ino Heitaro, causing all sorts of strange occurrences.

Chijiko

Surprising!
Nothing but an ordinary ball!

Data File

♀ Unknown   ☀ Edo period?   📖 *Collection of Hyakumonogatari Tales*

✍ *Mari* are a type of colorful ball usually played with by young girls. They're made by wrapping cotton or plant fibers around a seashell core, then covering them with paper or cloth.

A prank that spawned a Yokai legend.

Long ago, there was a castle where stories were told of a Yokai *mari* ball called Chijiko. This Yokai appeared each night by the Otemon Gate. One night a young Samurai was walking by the gate, when sure enough a ball appeared. It bounced up and down, left and right, while making jingling noises.

The Samurai slashed it in half with his sword. It proved to be an ordinary *mari* ball with a bell inside. In fact, the ball was attached to a line, and was being made to move by someone on the other side of the gate.

There wasn't a lot for people to do back then. They had to make their own fun, and these kinds of pranks were popular.

Tsuchikorobi

Relative of the Tsuchinoko.

When written in kanji, the name of the cryptid Tsuchinoko means "child of a mallet." The name comes from it looking like a snake shaped like a round mallet. This bizarrely shaped creature has different regional variations.

In Misasa, Totori prefecture, there is the Tsuchikorobi (rolling mallet). This Yokai rolls down hills and bites the legs of anyone it hits. In some books, it is written with different kanji, meaning "earth-roller."

It seems like this version was created for a children's book. It's a fun story but not traditional folklore.

Data File

- ⚬ Misasa, Tohaku, Tottori prefecture
- ❋ Ancient to present?
- ▯ *New Edition: Yokai Discourse*
- ✎ A *tsuchi* or *yokotsuchi* is a mallet that looks like a cylinder attached to a handle. It is often used to soften fabrics and cotton.

Surprising!
Just a rolling mallet!

Nurarihyon

Surprising!
A Yokai that makes no sense!

Data File

- ⚲ Literature
- ✳ Unknown
- 📖 *Toriyama Sekien's Gazu Hyakki Complete Collection*
- ✐ The word *nurarihyon* comes from a saying meaning "the slipperier it is, the harder to catch." That has come to sum up this elusive and mysterious Yokai.

The Yokai Shogun

The Nurarihyon is a slippery, hard-to-catch Yokai that walks into people's houses and helps itself to their tea—at least that's what is said. Strangely, the creature is not found in any old texts. In the Edo period, Nurarihyon appeared on Yokai scrolls having only a name and an image. From the name, people probably imagined some sort of slippery Yokai.

Most stories of Nurarihyon come from modern children's books, which is the likely source. There are quite a few Yokai that appear to be ancient but are actually recent creations.

Neko Musume

She couldn't stop herself from licking men!

Neko Musume is a famous manga and anime character with an odd history. In Awanokuni (Modern day Tokushima prefecture), the daughter of a wealthy family had the strange habit of licking men. Because she was beautiful, they easily found her a husband. However, he fled after a single night when she wouldn't stop licking his face and feet. The girl's tongue was rough like a cat's, so they called her Neko Musume, meaning "cat daughter."

She may have just been an oddball, but her story appears in many Yokai collections, usually called the Nameonna or "licking woman."

Data File

⚲ Tokushima prefecture

✸ Edo period

📖 *Collection of Edo Period Kaidan and Yokai Ehon Maki*

✎ The Neko Musume story first appeared in the Edo period book *Picture Book of a Light Autumn Night Rain.*

Surprising!
A Yokai made into an anime character!

Bake Otafuku

Surprising!
A Yokai invented to make money!

Data File

📍 Sakai, Chuo, Osaka-shikita, Osaka prefecture

☀ Meiji period

📓 *Study of Traditions Native to the Kansai Area*, Vol. 33

✎ An *otafuku* mask is a kind of lucky charm with a plump woman's face. Bake Otafuku is also known as Okame or Ofuku.

A Yokai in an *otafuku* mask?

There were rumors of a Bake Otafuku appearing on Tenjin Bridge in Osaka during the Meji period. At night a woman carrying a ladle with a face like an *otafuku* mask appeared, dancing and singing in a low voice "blessings for a bountiful year!"

Crowds began to gather every night hoping to catch a glimpse of her. Entrepreneurs set up night stalls to sell food to the onlookers.

Eventually, the police investigated and determined the owners of the stalls had set the whole thing up, starting the rumors to gather crowds in order to increase sales.

Honade

Touching cheeks on dark, lonely nights.

The Honade legend comes from Yamanashi prefecture and Okutama, Tokyo. It tells of travelers walking down lonely streets at night and feeling something brushing lightly against their cheeks. Okutama is underwater now because of a dam, but Honade stories persist.

One day, a young man set out to solve the mystery of the Honade. Sure enough, at night he felt something gently touching his cheek. On closer examination, he discovered his cheeks were damp with night dew from brushing against the pampas grass.

In the era before street lamps, there were many such occurences that were blamed on Yokai.

Surprising!
A spooky Yurei that's actually nothing more than pampas grass!

Data File

📍 Okutama, Nishitama, Tokyo ☀ Beginning Showa period?

📕 *Urban Legends of Okutama*

✍ Honade legends are old told in Doshi, Minamitsuru, Fujioshida, Yamanashi prefecture.

Yadokai

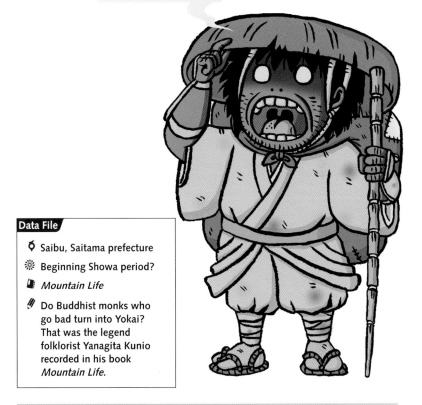

Surprising!
It's not even a real Yokai!

Data File

- Saibu, Saitama prefecture
- Beginning Showa period?
- *Mountain Life*
- Do Buddhist monks who go bad turn into Yokai? That was the legend folklorist Yanagita Kunio recorded in his book *Mountain Life*.

Yokai monks that sneak into homes at night?

Yadokai wear dirty white robes, with dirty socks and straw sandals. They sneak into people's houses, going through windows and rear doors, and snatch away children who don't listen to their parents.

Yadokai are usually described as monks on pilgrimages. When night fell, they would wander the streets shouting "Yadoka?" (Do you have a shed?") To some these eerie voices in the night sounded like Yokai.

Whether this explanation is true or not, nobody knows.

Yogore Hacho

A mysterious Yokai with an murky past.

The Yogore Hacho appears at night in Nagasaki prefecture. Other than that, nothing else is known about this Yokai's origin.

It may not be a Yokai at all but instead the aural phenomenon called *yogoe haccho* ("eight ward night voices.") This basically means that on quiet nights, even a whisper can carry as far as eight city wards (2,861 feet/872 meters). Seemingly, someone heard unidentified voices out of nowhere and thought it was a Yokai.

And so a scary Yokai was born from what is essentially an echo.

Surprising!
Voices that echo through the streets!

Data File

◊ Nagasaki prefecture   ☀ Ancient to Showa period?

📖 *Comprehensive Vocabulary of Japanese Folklore*

✒ This Yokai was probably used to frighten children into good behavior. "If you don't do as you're told, the Yogore Hacho will get you!"

Believe it or not, Yokai can die. Either they are killed or somehow die by their own hands. There are many ways for a Yokai
to die but surely these are the most ridiculous deaths.

CHAPTER

6

The Shameful Dead

Iwana Bozu

A kind Yokai protecting his friends to the end.

Just as there are Kitsune and Tanuki who take human form, there are also fish that shapeshift into people. Long ago, at Sankanbu in Gifu prefecture, there was an *iwana*, or arctic char, which transformed into a person.

A group of young people were fishing in a mountain river. They were fishing in the traditional method of spreading poison into the water to kill the fish. A monk they had never seen before came up to them and began to preach to them about why they shouldn't kill fish so indiscriminately.

Not in the mood for a lecture, they gave the monk some food to shut him up and tactfully took their leave. The next day they went fishing again in the same spot and pulled an enormous *iwana* from the river.

Surprising!

A yokai who gets
stuffed to the gills
and killed!

Data File

⚲ Ena, Gifu prefecture   ☀ Edo period

📖 *Historical Collection of the Lives of Japanese Common People*, Volume 16

🪶 Poison fishing used ground pepper plants that were poisonous only to the
fish. Fishermen scattered the poison in the water and grabbed the dead fish
when they floated to the surface.

When they cut the *iwana's* belly to clean it, the food they gave
the monk the day before came bursting out. The *iwana* was the
lord of the river and had transformed into a monk in order to protect his fellow fishy friends. But relaxed and stuffed from the feast
he had eaten, he fell victim to the poison floating in the water. He
was, after all, just a fish.

There are similar legends in the mountains of Tokyo and
Fukushima prefecture. Instead of *iwana*, they tell of *yamame*, or
Formosan salmon, and even *unagi* eels. No matter the fish, they
transform into a human and are inevitably killed.

They're Yokai, but you can't help feeling sorry for them.

Ningyo of Omi

Three mummified Merfolk.

The river Sakuragawa flows through Gamoteramachi, Higashi-omi in Shiga prefecture. It is crossed by the Teramura-bashi Bridge. Long ago there was a small pool upstream called Koshogafuchi. Some Ningyo, or Merfolk, lived there.

Three Ningyo siblings often took human form, and sometimes did chores at nearby Amadera temple. Unfortunately, they weren't great at keeping their human shapes and were caught.

One was sold from person to person, until bought by someone and was turned into a mummy for display. Another barely escaped and made it as far as Kono in Hino. They were captured there and died. The last fled to nearby Koya-san where the monk Kobo Daishi showed mercy. He lived at Karukaya-do, where he eventually died and was also eventually turned into a mummy.

Data File

◊ Gamoteramachi, Higashi-omi, Shiga prefecture

※ Heian period?　　📕 *A Walk with Japan's Yokai*

✎ Kobo Daishi, also known as Kukai, was the founder of the Shingon sect of Buddhism. He lived during the Heian period, and his is famous for establishing Koya-san in Wakayama prefecture as the base of Shingon Buddhism.

Surprising!
In happier days the merfolk helped out at a local temple!

The first mummy is still on display at Kanjo-ji temple in Kawai, Higashi-omi. The third Ningyo mummy is in Karukaya-do on Koya-san. And the second is said to be buried in the Merfolk's mound, or Ningyotzuka, in Kono, Hino.

If they had never been discovered by humans, the three Ningyo siblings probably would have led happy lives. But all of their endings were sad.

Ohaguro Baba

Her black teeth can been seen even in the dark.

Daitoku-ji in Kyoto is an ancient Zen Buddhist temple. Many years ago, there was a pine forest near the gate, and there lived the Yokai Ohaguro Baba.

The old Yokai diligently colored her teeth black, and even though it was dark in the forest, her teeth could still be seen. Ohaguro Baba's favorite thing to do was to frighten travelers.

One night, a blind nun decided that she had enough of the Ohaguro Baba. She prepared a large bag of food and headed to Daitoku-ji. Sure enough, the Ohaguro Baba turned her face towards the solitary traveler but being blind the nun was not startled at all. Still looking for a way to shock the stoic nun, the Ohaguro Baba drew closer. She smelled the food in the bag and, unable to resist, climbed inside.

The nun then sprang her trap and pulled the bag shut. Inside, the Ohaguro Baba revealed her true form as an ancient Tanuki. The nun thoroughly chastised the Tanuki for its unruly behavior.

Data File

- ⚲ Murakita-no-datoku-ji, Kita, Kyoto, Kyoto prefecture.
- ※ Ending Edo period
- 📖 *Local Pastimes*, Vol. 17
- ✎ In the Edo period, the custom was for women to dye their teeth black upon marriage. They soaked their teeth in a solution of iron-infused vinegar.

Surprising!
She couldn't resist
the tasty food!

The Shameful Dead

Kubitsuri Tanuki

Surprising!

A Tanuki that sacrificed itself to save a woman's life!

Data File

- Ikedachi, Miyoshi, Tokushima prefecture
- Beginning Showa period? *Tanuki Tales of Awa*
- The story of a suicidal Tanuki first appeared in Negishi Yasumori's book *Mimi Bukuro*.

A good deed from a suicidal yokai.

Kubitsuri Tanuki is a Yokai from Ikedachi, Miyoshi in Tokushima prefecture. It uses its powers to mesmerize people and make them hang themselves. As a result, enchanted people often hung themselves in Yutani Valley in Ikedachi. People who lived nearby felt something unnatural about the place and avoided it as much as possible.

Along with that sinister monster, there are other Kubitsuri Tanuki in Edo. Around what is now Yushima, Bunkyo, a young man and woman were preparing to commit double suicide. They hung themselves, and while the woman died, the man's rope was longer and he lived. Just then, the woman who supposedly killed herself came walking up. It turns out, the one who died was a Tanuki who had taken her shape.

It seems that the Tanuki had overheard the two talking about how their parents refused to allow them to marry, so they planned to unite in the next world. The Tanuki decided to save the woman and die in her place. Hearing this story, their parents consented to their marriage.

No one knows why the Tanuki did this. Maybe it heard them talking and took pity on them.

Kodama Nezumi

Data File

◊ Akita prefecture   ※ Ancient to present?

📖 *Memoirs of an Akita Winter Hunter*

✏ *Matagi* are traditional winter hunters in the mountains of eastern Japan. They hunt together in groups using one of the three traditional methods: *shigeno* (heavy fields), *aoba* (blue leaves), or *kodama* (small ball).

Surprising!
It explodes if the mountain Kami is in a bad mood!

Yokai that used to be ordinary hunters.

In Akita prefecture, the hunters called *matagi* sometimes hear strange sounds in the mountains. If they hear a sound like an explosion, they know they must leave the mountain immediately

The explosive sound signals the mountain Kami deity is in a foul mood. The hunters know they will take no prey and possibly suffer accidents caused by the grumpy Kami.

The heralds of the bad mood are Kodama Nezumi. They can cause explosions from their backs, which is the sound the hunters hear. It's said they were once *matagi* hunters who hunted in the traditional *kodama* style. Legend says a woman mountain Kami came to the mountain shelter of the kodama *matagi* hunters asking for help with a pregnancy. The men refused. The mountain Kami then cursed them and turned them into mice.

Now whenever the Kami is is a bad mood, it summons the Kodama Nezumi from their holes in the trees so they can use their explosive abilities. Even though the mountain Kami was angered, I still think this was a little cruel.

Konaki Baba

Are you going to eat that?

Many people in Japan are familiar with the Yokai Konaki Jiji. Found in Tokushima prefecture, it looks like a baby with the face of an old man. Konaki Jiji cries like a baby, fooling passersby into thinking it is an abandoned infant. They pick it up to hold it, and the tricky Yokai grows heavier and heavier. Eventually the people are crushed to death under its weight.

The book *A Journey through Tohoku Kaidan* also tells of a Konaki Baba. The story tells of someone lost in the mountains in the Tsugaru region of Aomori prefecture. He meets an old man, who offers to bring him to his house and help.

Along the way, they find two infants in the woods. Looking closely, the babies have the faces of old women. When they get to his house, the old man throws the babies in a pot of boiling water and closes the lid. When the lid is lifted again, there are two pumpkins being boiled.

The following morning, the wanderer is told "Those pumpkins you ate last night were Konaki Baba."

That's the whole story...a Yokai that turns into a pumpkin in boiling water. I have no idea if Konaki Baba are related to Konaki Jiji in any way.

Surprising!
It turns into a pumpkin when boiled!

Data File

⚲ Tsuguru area, Aomori prefecture

✳ Edo period?

📖 *A Journey through Tohoku Kaidan*

🖊 In Hiroshima prefecture there is a Yokai called Kabochakoro, which is basically a large, rolling pumpkin. But in fact, pumpkin Yokai are rare.

Konnyaku Bo

Data File

◊ Wakayama prefecture ※ Around Edo period?

▬ *Obake Stories of Kishu*

✎ It takes about two to three years before a *konnyaku* yam can be harvested. If it grows longer than that, the yam gets massive and turns into a Konnyaku Bo.

A Yokai who loves taking baths?

Konnyaku Bo appears in a Wakayama book of fairy takes. They are *konnyaku* yams that have grown too large and take on human shape. For some reason, they love taking baths. This is their story.

A *konnyaku* yam that had transformed into a Konnyaku Bo stopped by a local temple every night. He looked like an average traveling monk and being hospitable, the temple allowed him to use their bath.

When the monk took his bath, he would aways say the same odd thing, "Good thing there's no ashes in the bath!" One day the abbot of the temple decided to test him by putting ashes in the bath. When the traveling monk did not come out of the bathing room, the abbot was worried and went into look. There was a huge *konnyaku* yam floating in the water bucket.

The abbot had an idea and built a large fire under the tub. Sure enough, as the water boiled several *konnyaku* yams bubbled up to the surface.

When *konnyaku* is prepared for eating, it's boiled in water with ashes to remove the bitterness. The Konnyaku Bo revealed his own weakness.

Nisekisha

Kitsune and Tanuki transformed into phantom trains.

Train lines were first built in Japan around the Meiji period. There were often reports by train drivers and people who lived near the tracks of the sound of trains when there was nothing there. People would hear steam engines or whistles blowing at night when no trains were running.

At the time, only a single train ran along a track. Train drivers reported seeing the light of an oncoming train suddenly appear. Trying to avoid a crash, they would pull the breaks hard, but the trains would be moving too fast. However, just when it appeared that the trains would crash into each other, the oncoming train vanished.

These phantom trains were Kitsune and Tanuki. Fascinated by these strange new machines crossing the land, they used their shapeshifting powers to prank people. They played their usual pranks of trying to startle the train drivers. Sadly, they were often struck by the oncoming train. They got so into their game they forget to jump out of the way.

Data File

⚲ Nationwide

❋ Beginning Showa period?

▯ *Modern Folktales*, Volume 3

⫰ Kensho-ji temple in Kameari, Katsushika, Toky,o has a burial mound for a Tanuki killed as it posed as a phantom train. It transformed into a steam train on the Joban line.

Hitotsume Tanuki

It makes its eye bigger to shock people!

Long ago, there was a mountain pass in Tonda, Shirahama, Wakayama prefecture called Hitomezaka, meaning "Slope of the Single Eye." It was named for a local Yokai. A Tanuki lived on this mountain pass, and it loved to play tricks on travelers.

This Tanuki was the Hitotsume Tanuki, or one-eyed Tanuki. It had a single eye in the middle of its head. It could enlarge its own eye. When travelers went over the pass at night, it would appear and enlarge its eye. When people saw the massive orb, they would run away in fright.

Once a blind masseuse was traveling the pass. The Hitotsume Tanuki appeared and played its usual trick. However, the masseuse didn't respond. Stubborn to the last, the Hitotsume Tanuki made his eye bigger and bigger until it was too big for its own head and popped out. The momentum made the Tanuki fall backwards, where it hit its head and died.

The Hagruo Baba of Kyoto met a similar end. Blind people are the natural enemies of Yokai who like to startle people.

Data File

⚲ Tonda, Shirahama, Wakayama prefecture   ❀ Pre-Showa era?

📕 *Obake Stories of Kishu*

✎ The old Hitomezaka ("Slope of the Single Eye") mountain pass in Tonda named after the Hitotsume Tanuki is now closed. Today, Highway 42, runs through a tunnel under the pass.

Surprising!

If its eye gets too big, it can die!

Farai Neko

Actually a Kitsune ghost?

Farai Neko look like ordinary cats, but they have the ability to possess people. They are especially known for possessing babies. Possessed children will inexplicably break out in a fever, one that cannot be cured no matter how many times they are taken to the doctor.

Data File

◊ Gotenba, Shizuoka prefecture   ✳ Ancient to Taisho era

▥ *History of Shizuoka Prefecture*, Vol. 24: Folktales

✎ The *farai* in Farai Neko refers to a wind that comes out of nowhere, but it might also be related to *furai*, meaning erratic.

The only way to cure the sickness is to expel the Farai Neko. To do that, you put a special trap by the backdoor. Any cats caught in the trap that cry are normal cats. They can be let go. Farai Neko never cry out.

Once the Yokai cat has been identified, the family and relatives of the sick child must get together then boil and eat it. This will cause its spirit to leave the baby.

Farai Neko are often shown to actually be Kitsune ghosts. The dead Kitsune's spirit possess the cat, and then moves into the baby. It's a complicated process. Somehow the Kitsune is still linked to the cat's body, and killing it ends the evil and cures the baby.

Surprising!
A Yokai boiled in a pot and eaten!

Maikubi

Three flying heads!

The Edo period book *Night Stories of Tosanjin*, the Maikubi appear in the sea off the Manatzuru Peninsula in Kanagawa prefecture.

During the Kamakura period, three former criminals became officials of the Kamakura shogunate. Kosanda, Matashige, and Akugoro were all rough characters. They met at a shrine festival in Manatzuru.

At first, they all got along drinking but tensions flared and swords were drawn. First, Akugoro cut off Kosanda's head. The other two chased and chased each other until they fell into the ocean. In a calm between the waves the two attacked and cut each other's heads off at the same time. Normally things would end there.

However, their two severed heads continued the battle, eventually joined by Kosanda's head. Fire came from their mouths and they bit each other's necks.

The three heads kept fighting, noon and night. They looked like pinwheel fireworks and were, disappointingly, not very scary.

Data File

◊ Manatzuru, Ashigarashimo, Kanagawa prefecture

❀ Kamakura period

▨ *Night Stories of Tosanjin / Ehon Hyakumonogatari*

✐ According to *Night Stories of Tosanjin*, the three heads circle around Tomoe Pond. But in modern terms we do not know where that is.

Surprising!

Three heads that fight each other!

Yama Jiji

The old Yokai man of the Shikoku Mountains.

Yama Jiji, also known as Yama Chichi, live in the mountains of the island of Shikoku. Some look like regular human beings, but Edo period records talk about Yama Jiji that are only a foot tall or have a single leg. Other writings say they have one eye so small it looks like they have only a single, large eye. They feed on forest creatures. It's said even wolves fear Yama Jiji.

If it sounds terrifying, there are some fun Yama Jiji as well. Some became friends with humans. A legend from Monobechi, Kami, in Kochi prefecture tells of a person who befriended a Yama Jiji. The farmer had millet seeds that guaranteed an abundant harvest when planted. At the end of every year, the Yama Jiji came by to eat mochi made from the millet.

Every year, the Yama Jiji ate more and more mochi. Deciding enough was enough, one year the farmer fed the Yama Jiji heated stones instead of mochi. With his throat burning, the Yama Jiji begged for tea. The farmer gave him oil to drink.

His throat burned and the Yama Jiji died. But his curse lingered, and the famer's house and status declined. In this story, humans are meaner than Yokai!

Data File

⬦ Shikoku

✳ Showa period?

📖 *Legends of Tosa*

✎ Millet is a type of grain, commonly used to make dumplings including mochi a favorite snack of the Yama Jiji.

Raiju

Yokai that ride storm clouds.

When lightning strikes, there are those who are enervated and flit around between heaven and earth. The creatures called Raiju appeared all over the country.

Raiju look something like a dog or Tanuki. They ride storm clouds and occasionally, accidentally fall to the ground. Raiju who fall to earth look to return to the skies. We have records of some who were captured by humans.

Some tried to keep them as pets. Many were mummified and displayed. Those mummies can still be seen across the country.

Surprising!
Some have been captured and mummified!

Data File

⚲ Throughout Japan   ☀ Beginning Showa period?

📖 *Animal Yokai Collection*, Vol. 1

🖊 Several temples have Raiju mummies, such as Yuzan-ji in Hanamaki, Iwate prefecture and Sai-ji in Nakaoka, Nigata prefecture.

Some Yokai are a joke. Some are just funny looking. These Yokai never had a chance. The best you can say about them is they are...unique.

CHAPTER

7

Unique Yokai

Ichiku Tachiku Kozo

Unknown kid singing a happy song.

A Yokai of unknown appearance wanders the Senba area of Chuo, Osaka. Senba was known for having short trenches, about six feet (1.8 meters) long used for water run-off. One still remains at the intersection of Awajimachidori and Dobuikesuji.

Data File

📍 Chuo, Osaka, Osaka prefecture   ☀ Meiji period

📖 *Folklore – Traditions and History*, Vol. 26, No. 2

✏ Ichiku Tachiku was an Edo period nursery song. In the Meiji period, candy sellers sang it to attract customers. They sang and walked in a clownish way, and the song became a big hit.

Surprising!
A Yokai whose name comes from a popular Meiji period song!

A mysterious child's voice was heard in Senba at night. It sang , "Ichiku, tachiku, Mr. Taemon. A chingaramon is right behind you!" It skipped audibly across the trench in time with the song. Because it was so dark, no one ever saw the singer.

No children would be playing that late. Scared of the unknown voice, people in the neighborhood said it was a Yokai, and named it Ichiku Tachiku Kozo.

The song the Ichiku Tachiku Kozo sang was a version of the Edo period nursery rhyme "Ichiku Tachiku." It is still sung today in nurseries and preschools.

Oshimearai Yurei

The sad Yurei of women who died in chldbirth.

Long ago in the Yukigaya area of Ota, Tokyo, there was a statue of the Bodhisattva Jizo called Oshime Jizo, or Diaper Jizo. The story says it was put there because of a spectral woman suddenly appeared to travelers at night and demanded they wash her baby's dirty diapers.

We know very little about this Yokai. The primary source doesn't say more than "it appears." Of course, when talking about a ghostly woman saying "it appears" is scary enough.

Villagers called this strange spirit Oshimearai Yurei, and raised the Oshime Jizo as a memorial, hoping to soothe her troubled soul.

Creepy name aside, the Oshimearai Yurei seems to be a type of Ubume (page 80). Ubume are the Yurei of women who died in childbirth. They appear in water or on roadways and ask people to hold their baby.

In Fukue, Hagi, Yamaguchi prefecture, there are stories of Ubume who carry their babies on their backs and wash diapers in a lake. Given that, it seems likely Oshimearai Yurei are a type of Ubume.

Data File

◊ Yukigawa, Ota, Kyoto prefecture ☀ Ancient to Taisho period

▯ *Cultural Assets of Ota*, Vol. 22: Oral literature

✎ Oshime means "children's diapers." Unlike modern disposable diapers, the diapers of the period were long strips of cloth that needed to be washed.

Surprising!
A Yokai that asks people to wash dirty diapers!

Shiriko Boshi

An evil monster who only targets butts.

On the Kii peninsula, Kappa are often called such-and-such Koboshi, or such-and-such Boshi. Boshi is a term for Buddhist priests, but here it is meant to mean a small child. Like calling a kid "young master."

In Shima, Mie prefecture, Kappa are referred to as Shiriko Boshi. Shiriko means "butt child," because this Kappa goes straight for the butt. They crave the elusive *shirikodama*, a mythical organ said to reside in the rear end of humans. Shiriko Boshi put their hands up people's butts and attempt to tear out these organs.

Besides rivers and lakes, Kappa also hunt in the ocean. Children swimming in the sea and the women called *ama* who dive for turban shells and abalone are terrified of the Shiroko Boshi.

Depending on the area, some days are more dangerous than others. In Fuseda, Shima, Shiroko Boshi are most active during the Tenno Matsuri festival. Going into the water during this festival is very risky.

Data File

⬥ Shima, Mie prefecture

※ Ancient to Showa period?

▦ *The Ama of Shima*

✎ The Tenno Matsuri is held on June 14th of the lunar calendar. The festival celebrates Emperor Gozu as the kami Susano no mikoto. It more often takes place mid-July in modern times.

If someone must go into the water during the Tenno Matsuri, they tie a branch of *sansho* peppers around their neck like a necklace. This keeps the Shiroko Boshi away.

Surprising!
"Butt child" is right in its name!

Sema

Data File

- ⚲ Nakijin, Kunigami, Okinawa prefecture
- ☀ Ancient to Showa period?
- 📖 *Southeastern Studies*, Vol. 19
- ✎ There are varied similar legends with different names; Kijimuna, Kimuya, Bunagaya, Akaganta, Handanmi, Michibata, Yakanna.

Horrific Yokai of Graveyard Island.

On Okinawa there are Yokai called Kijimuna. They are said to be tree spirits of banyan and Japanese sea fig trees. They look like children with bright red hair and bodies. They love mischief, such as tormenting sleeping people, or making people go in circles on roads at night.

Kijimuna legends are told all over the Okinawan islands, and most of them are good fun. However, there are regional variations with different names and personalities. They are a complicated Yokai.

Off the Haneji inland sea in Nakijin, there's a deserted island called Yaganna. The Kjimuna on this island are called Sema. There are male and female varieties.

Since long ago people have avoided Yaganna. Anyone who breaks this taboo and lands on the island is immediately captured by Sema. The male and female Sema will suffocate their victims.

It's no wonder Sema's name means evil spirit.

Tanukibi

A flaming cow and person all in one!

When Kitsune spark mysterious fires they are called Kitsunebi. Likewise, when Tanuki light fires they are called Tanukibi.

Sometimes Tanukibi are strung out like the lights of a funeral procession. Sometimes they imitate the blaze of an agricultural burn. In the Edo period book *Shokoku Rijindan*, or *Village Tales from Many Countries*, there is an unusual tale of Tanukibi.

The story comes from what is now Higashitada, Kawanishi in Hyogo prefecture. There was a road so twisty it was called the Eel Path. Tanukibi often appeared on this road.

One night when rain was falling, a farmer walking the Eel Path saw a person leading a cow, with both of them on fire. Taking it in stride, the farmer pulled out a cigarette and asked the fiery person for a light. The man and his cow gladly obliged. This is an odd urban legend...

The man and the cow were actually a single Tanukibi. They didn't cause anyone any trouble, and as to why Tanuki would take that shape, I have no idea.

This apparition has nothing in common with fire Yokai. It's probably called a Tanukibi because it is a Tanuki shapeshifting into a flaming human.

Data File

⬦ Higashitada, Kawanishi, Hyogo prefecture

✳ Edo period

📖 *Complete Essays of Japan, New Edition*, Vol. 2, Book 24

〽 Agricultural burning is controlled burning of grasslands and forests, then using the ash as fertilizer. This was practiced in the mountain villages of Shikoku until the middle of the Showa period.

Domo Komo

Modeled after genius doctors?

Domo Komo is a Yokai created during the Edo period. It was drawn in picture scrolls called *emaki*. It had only a name and an appearance, with no backstory.

With two heads springing from a single neck, what kind of Yokai could they even be? But it was a cool character design, so artists kept using it.

There is an old Mukashi Banashi that might have something to do with this Yokai. Once upon a time, there were two genius doctors, Domo (ferocious) and Komo (wise). They competed to see who was the best doctor in Japan.

To start, Domo cut off Komo's head and reattached it. Komo then did the same for Domo. They then decided they would cut off each other's heads and whoever could reattach their own head was the winner. With both their heads cut off, neither was able to reattach anything and they both died.

The result of the Domo-Komo contest looks nothing like this Yokai, but its highly likely that story inspired an artist to draw this strange Yokai.

Data File

⬡ Emakimono   ❋ Unknown

📘 *Survey of Japan's Mukashi Banashi*, Vol. 21: Tokushima and Kagawa

✏ Domo Komo are found in Oda Gosumi's *Hyakki Yagyo Emaki* and Hokusai Suechika's *Bakemono Tsukushi Emaki* picture scrolls.

Surprising!

A Yokai that's neither
this nor that!

Chanchaka Obaba

An old woman nestled in a toilet

Kitami-do is a temple in Osaka. During the Meiji period, children often played on the grounds. There was a rumor that a Yokai lived in the toilet furthest in the back.

This Yokai, called Chanchaka Obaba, was an old woman with tangled white hair. There's no story of this Yokai actually doing anything, but in the evening, children would chant in front of the toilet, "Chanchaka Obaba! Red paper or white paper?" The children would then run away without waiting for an answer.

There's nothing scary about the Chanchaka Obaba, not even her name. But it seems kids had fun being scared.

Surprising!
A Yokai without a scary name!

Data File

⚲ Honmachi, Chuo, Osaka, Osaka prefecture

❀ Meiji period

📖 *Folklore – Traditions and History*, Vol. 26, No. 2

✐ Kitami-do is a branch temple of Hongan-ji. The toilet where Chanchaka Obaba lived was destroyed in WWII. It was between the main gate and the entertainment quarters.

Nakanishi

Surprising!
A Yokai with a regular human name!

Data File

- Naha, Okinawa prefecture
- Meiji to beginning Showa
- *Local Customs Research*, Vol. 5, No. 2
- There is still a bridge in Naha called Shiowatari, but the old wooden bridge Nakanishi appeared on was further north.

Don't call its name!

Nakanishi appeared on the Shiowatari bridge, which spanned the Katabaru salt pans, a pond used for drying sea water for salt. At night, if you called "Hey Nakanishi!" while standing on this bridge, the Yokai would come and take the person who called his name.

People taken by Nakanishi were usually found later dazed, sitting in a pond or a well in the back of a cave.

Why anyone would summon this Yokai by calling its name at night, or what Nakanishi looks like, or any other information about it are unknown. There are quite a few Yokai mysteries.

Biron

Is this really a Yokai?

Biron was introduced in Sato Arifumi's books *Field Guide to Japan's Yokai* and *Yokai Great Field Guide*. It says the Yokai is sometimes called Nuribotoke and hides inside Buddhist altars inside people's homes.

The books report this was a Yokai that tried to transform into a Buddha with the incantation "Biro, Biro, Birooon." But it failed and was stuck in this form. Sprinkling salt on it will make it go away.

This story doesn't appear in any other record. Biron appears on *emaki* and other illustrations, but this explanation comes only from the author's imagination.

Data File

6 Unknown

※ Unknown

The Most Complete Japanese Yokai Field Guide

Biron is also known as Nuribotoke and appears in Edo period yokai *emaki* and pictures books. It's usually drawn as a human shaped creature with its eyeballs hanging out. But there is no other explanation.

Surprising!
Not much thought put into this yokai!

Buriburi

It's named after the way it sounds.

Its name sounds like something that might come dribbling out your butt, but it is actually the sound of a pestle grinding in a mortar.

In Ino, Kochi prefecture, the sound of a pestle grinding in a mortar can be heard deep in the mountains when no one is around. The sound, "buriburiburi," gives the yokai Buriburi its name. Buriburi are invisible, but they do have bodies. They sometimes smash into people when rushing around.

It's creepy to think about this invisible monster flying around the forests making that sound. However, because Buriburi go in a straight line, they are easy to avoid. When you hear their distinctive sound, lie down face first, and the yokai will pass over you harmlessly.

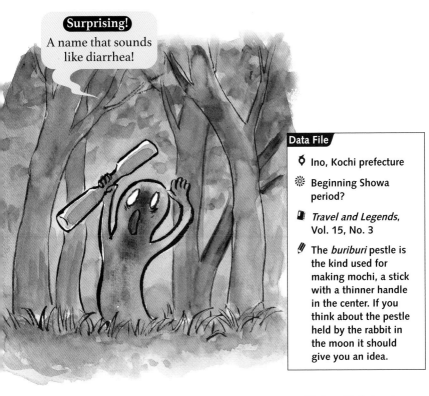

Surprising!
A name that sounds like diarrhea!

Data File

⚲ Ino, Kochi prefecture

✳ Beginning Showa period?

📖 *Travel and Legends*, Vol. 15, No. 3

✎ The *buriburi* pestle is the kind used for making mochi, a stick with a thinner handle in the center. If you think about the pestle held by the rabbit in the moon it should give you an idea.

Fundoshibi

Underwear-shaped Hitodama.

Human souls that slip free from their bodies form the shape of flaming balls and float around. These are called Hitodama. Most of these are spirits of the dead, those who died of illness or accidents.

Most Hitodama have a small tail that trails behind them. In Nara prefecture, there is a Hitodama whose tails stretches very far behind them, called the Fundoshibi.

The Gundoshibi gets its name because its long tail looks like a flaming *fundoshi* (undergarment) that has been washed and hung out to dry.

Data File

- ◊ Nara prefecture
- ✳ Beginning Showa period?
- 📖 *Travel and Legends*, Vol. 8, Number 5
- ✎ Fundoshi are a single strip of cloth wrapped as a loincloth and used as underwear by men. There are regional and occupational variations, such as Ecchu Fundoshi and Rokushaku Fundoshi.

Surprising!
Its long tail makes it look like underwear!

Mikoshi Yurei

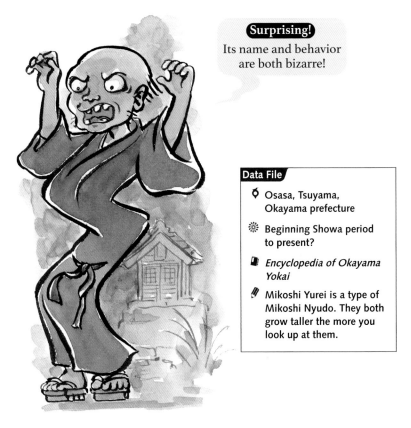

Surprising!
Its name and behavior
are both bizarre!

Data File

- 📍 Osasa, Tsuyama, Okayama prefecture

- ☀ Beginning Showa period to present?

- 📖 *Encyclopedia of Okayama Yokai*

- 🖊 Mikoshi Yurei is a type of Mikoshi Nyudo. They both grow taller the more you look up at them.

It folds into thirds with a clicking sound.

In Tsuyama, Okayama prefecture, there is a road near Lake Hinouchi that is dark even during the day. Along the road is an old shrine, where the Mikoshi Yurei appears.

A large man appears suddenly before people walking the road at night. As travelers look up at him, he rapidly increases in size. With a clicking sound, it's body bends in three parts, like an accordion. The Mikoshi Yurei has that extra surprise to startle travelers even more.

Rojin no Hi

Looks like an old man in front of a campfire.

This Yokai comes from the Edo period book *Night Stories of Tosanjin*. They appeared on rainy nights, in the mountains that form a border between Nagano and Shizuoka prefectures.

At first glance, it looks like nothing more than an old man huddling around a burning campfire. In fact, the fire and the old man are a single Yokai.

As evidence, if you try to burn meat in the fire, both the fire and old man disappear. Does the old man make the fire, or does the fire make the old man? There is no way to ever tell.

Surprising!
Is this Yokai the fire or the old man?

Data File

⚲ The boundary of Nagano and Shizuoka prefectures

❈ Edo period?

▣ *Night Stories of Tosanjin / Ehon Hyakumonogatari*

✐ The fire of a Rojin No Hi grows larger if you put water on it, the opposite of normal fires. In the Edo period these were also called Inka.

Uma Shika

Neither a deer nor a horse.

Uma Shika is another Yokai with a name and appearance that appeared in Edo period *emaki* picture scrolls. It doesn't look like either a deer or a horse. Instead, it looks like a weird person with a ridiculous facial expression. The term "horse deer" (baka) means "idiot" in Japanese, and this is probably an artist's idea of what such a person would look like.

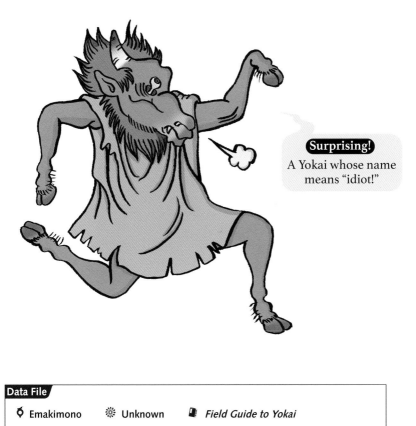

Surprising!
A Yokai whose name means "idiot!"

Data File

🜨 Emakimono   ☀ Unknown   📖 *Field Guide to Yokai*

✎ The Umashika and Gotaimen appear in Oda Gosumi's *Hyakki Yagyo Emaki*. They record only the name and appearance.

Gotaimen

Arms and legs attached to a giant head.

Gotaimen is an assemblage of the five parts of a human body—the head, both hands, both legs, gathered around the face. Since the five parts (*gotai*) are attached to the face (*men*), the Gotaimen is essentially a visualized pun, drawn by an artist as a Yokai.

Surprising!
A Yokai pun!

Data File

⚬ Emakimono

✳ Unknown

📖 *Field Guide to Yokai*

✎ In some cases, the five parts of the human body are the head, neck, chest, arms, and legs.

Nuppori Bozu

> **Surprising!**
> It shows you the eyeball in its butt!

A Yokai with an eyeball in its butt.

This Yokai appeared in what is now Katabiragatsuji, Ukyo, Kyoto. In recent times it is called Shirime. It's a type of faceless Nopperabo Yokai, with no eyes, ears, or mouth. This big difference is Nuppori Bozu have a giant eyeball in their butts. It shines with a light as bright as lightning.

Data File

- Ukyo, Kyoto, Kyoto prefecture
- Edo period?
- *Yokai Hyakumonogatari Emaki*
- Nuppori bozu was drawn by poet Yosa Bunson in his Yokai emaki picture scroll.

Unique Yokai

Tora Nyanya

> **Surprising!**
> A strange Yokai that loves money!

A weirdo born from Buddhist sutras.

A passage in a Buddhist sutra Nilakantha Dharanai chants "Tora ya- ya-." This yokai is a personified version of that chant. It has a tigerlike body with the face of a greedy monk. It loves money, so it hides inside wallets and places where money is kept.

Data File

- Emakimono
- Unknown
- *Yokai Hyakumonogatari Emaki*
- Zen is a Buddhist sect. Their temples are easily identifiable by their meditation training spaces.

Mappira

Mid-apology with its eyes up?

This Yokai was created by an anonymous *emakimono* scroll artist. "Mappira gomen" is used when begging for forgiveness. The Yokai Mappira is a personification of that phrase.

Data File

⚲ Emakimono ※ Unknown

🕮 *Field Guide to Yokai, Continued*

✎ In the Edo period, many Yokai in *emakimono* were based on puns.

Surprising!
A Yokai that looks like a kicked dog!

Surprising!
Never getting the whole picture!

Data File

⚲ Emakimono ※ Unknown

🕮 *Field Guide to Yokai, Continued*

✎ Yokai made from puns often have no commentary. They are images imagined from words.

Nannjyaka

What even is this?

The same anonymous artist that created Mappira created this Yokai as well in a Yokai *emaki* picture scroll. It depicts the middle part of the human body. No one knows that this is supposed to be. There is a sort of tail, so maybe it's an animal mid-transformation?

Boroboro Ton

A ragged old futon?

During the Edo period, ukiyo-e artist Toriyama Sekien created many Yokai through wordplay. Boroboro were a type of begging monks also called *komuso*, whose name sounded like "boroboro" meaning "ragged." Toriyama put the two together to make this Yokai.

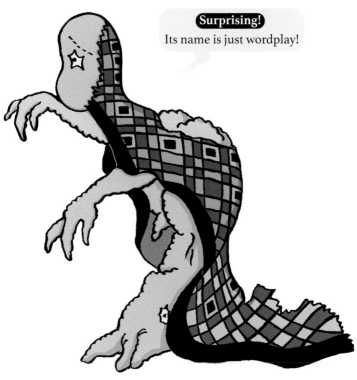

Surprising!
Its name is just wordplay!

Data File

♀ Literature　　※ Unknown

📖 *Toriyama Sekien's Gazu Hyakki Complete Collection*

✒ Komuso were a type of monk who wandered through town playing the *shakuhachi* flute begging for alms.

Yamaoroshi

A metal grater Obake!

Yamaoroshi is another Yokai created by Toriyama Sekien. Metal graters were used for grating vegetables like *daikon*. Toriyama basically looked at the graters, thought of porcupines, and imagined this Yokai.

Surprising!
A kitchen tool and a porcupine!

Data File

○ Literature ※ Unknown

📖 *Toriyama Sekien's Gazu Hyakki Complete Collection*

✏ Porcupines did not exist in Japan, but Edo period people knew of them from books.

Amabie is the most famous, but there are a host of future-telling Yokai who predict diseases, disasters, and harvests. When you take a close look at them, they are all rather disappointing.

CHAPTER

8

Yokai Prophets

Amabie

Became famous during the Covid pandemic.

Data File

- ◊ Thought to be from Kumamoto prefecture
- ✵ Thought to be from the Edo period
- 📖 *Encyclopedia of Japanese Phantom Beasts*
- ✏ Fake News is a term for misinformation spread via television, newspapers, and social media.

Surprising!
Copying the image doesn't say anything about curing disease!

Amabiko

Three-footed monster who prophesized a plague.

Amabie appeared in the ocean off Kumamoto during the Edo period. It spoke to a government official, predicting disease as well as a bumper crop. It disappeared into the water, saying "In time of plague, share my image!" This encounter was recorded in a *kawaraban* broadsheet.

Surprising!
Pretty much just Amabie!

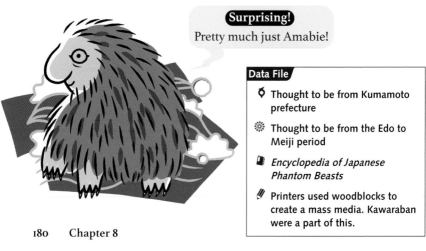

Data File

- ◊ Thought to be from Kumamoto prefecture
- ✵ Thought to be from the Edo to Meiji period
- 📖 *Encyclopedia of Japanese Phantom Beasts*
- ✏ Printers used woodblocks to create a mass media. Kawaraban were a part of this.

Arie

Surprising!

This cute yokai is the apex seamonster!

Data File

⚲ Thought to be from Kumamoto prefecture

✿ Thought to be from the Meiji period

▯ *Teito Yokai Newspaper*

∥ Korori is an infectious disease thought to be transmitted by vibrio cholerae. In modern times it is called cholera, but the Edo period it was known as *korori*.

This most powerful of sea creatures?

Kawaraban were the Edo period equivalent of broadside newspapers. Sensational and weird news sold well, so *kawaraban* often printed what we would call today "fake news."

Another Yokai found in *kawaraban* was the Amabiko, described as something like a three-footed monkey. Printers sometimes used different kanji for the Amabiko, sometimes using the character for "nun" and sometimes for "heaven." It also appeared off the coast of Kumamoto, predicting a coming plague followed by a bumper crop. The plague could be averted, it said, by copying and distributing its image.

The Amabie and Amabiko stories are exactly the same. Most think that one is simply a misspelling of the other, with the characters for "ko" and "e" being mixed up.

The Arie also appeared off the cost of Kumamoto, this time in the Meiji period. This creature actually came ashore and walked around town. Meeting a former Samurai, the Arie revealed he was the lord of all sea creatures. A disease similar to cholera would soon ravage the land and could only be averted by people copying the arie's image and venerating it morning and night. With that said, the strange creature returned to the sea.

Telling the same story as the Amabie and the Amabiko, the tale of the Arie spread and was widely believed.

Jinja Hime

Messenger from Ryugu.

Jinja Hime was a type of merfolk who appeared in the ocean off Nagasaki. Its body was 20 feet (six meters) long, it had horns on its head, and three swords spiked its tail.

The person who saw it said the Jinja Hime claimed to be a messenger from the undersea dragon's palace of Ryugu and prophesized seven years of abundant crops and korori epidemic. If its image was shared the epidemic could be averted.

Kamiike Hime (page 184) is an alternate version of the Jinja Hime. Its prophecy is the same, with the coming plague and sharing its image being the key to averting disaster. The biggest difference is the Kamiike Hime's body being longer, a staggering 33 feet (ten meters), and its three-sword tail is incorporated as part of its fins.

Surprising!
Swords in its tail for
no reason!

Data File

○ Thought to be from Nagasaki prefecture

✳ Thought to be from the Edo period

📖 *Encyclopedia of Japanese Phantom Beasts*

✒ The Jinja Hime was popular and its picture was copied and printed many times.

Hitokai

Entirely a snail!

Hitogai looks like a woman emerging from a massive snail shell. It is also known as the Kaidejin, or "shell-emerging person." It appeared in Fukshimagata, Nigata prefecture. Hitogai prophesized five years of good harvest followed by an ill wind. It followed with the same advice of how sharing its image could avert the disaster.

Honengame (page 184) arouse in the ocean off Kumano, Wakayama prefecture. It was 16 feet (five meters) long and looked like a turtle with a human face. There is no record of the honengame actually delivering a prophecy, but like the rest of the prophetic beasts the newspaper still claimed sharing its image would avert a coming epidemic.

Surprising!
A prophetic beast that tells no prophecy!

Data File

- ⚲ Thought to be from Nigata prefecture
- ☀ Thought to be from the Edo period
- 📖 *Encyclopedia of Japanese Phantom Beasts*
- ✎ Fukushima Bay is a lagoon in Kitaku, Nigata, Nigata prefecture. Long ago seawater flowed in with the ebb and and flow of the tides.

Kamiike Hime

A 33-foot- (ten-meter-) long merfolk!

Surprising!
Just copying the
Jinja Hime!

Data File

- ⚲ Thought to be from Nigata prefecture
- ☀ Thought to be from the Edo period
- 📖 *Illustrated Book of Medical Practices in Numazu in the Early Modern Period*
- ✎ The Kamike Hime image is hand drawn. It was preserved in an old house in Namazu, Shizuoka prefecture.

Honengame

A giant turtle!

Data File

- ⚲ Thought to be from Wakayama prefecture
- ☀ Thought to be from the Edo period
- 📖 *Encyclopedia of Japanese Phantom Beasts*
- ✎ There is another human-faced turtle called Kameona that appeared in Fukushima Bay and delivered the usual prophecy.

Surprising!
No one knows what it looks
like inside the shell!

Kudan

The ultimate prophetic beast!

An omen of a forthcoming disaster, be it war or infectious disease, is the birth of a human-faced cow. This is the prophetic beast Kudan.

As soon as they are born, the Kudan speak their prophecy. The next five years will see an abundant harvest followed by a terrible disease." Upon speaking their words, they die.

It's said that a Kudan prophecy always comes true. When one is born somewhere, word quickly spreads across the country.

During the Edo period, images of Kudan were used as amulets of protection against illness.

Surprising!
It dies right after telling its prophecy!

Data File

⚥ Western Japan

❀ Edo – Showa period

📖 *Folklore*, Vol. 2, No. 6

✎ Kudan often appear before the outbreak of war. One delivered its prophecy right before World War II.

Kutahe

Prophetic beast of Mt. Take, Toyama.

Kutahe, also called Kutabe, appear on the peak of Mt. Tate in Toyama prefecture. They have a human face on an animal's body.

During the Edo period, a Kutahe appeared before someone picking herbs on Mt. Tate. It spoke, "From now there will be some unknown illness, what it is I do not know. However, if you look upon my image even one time, you will not fall sick."

Basically, the same prophecy as the Amabie and Jinja Hime, but that didn't stop printers and illustrators from spreading the story.

Surprising!
It can't even predict the disease's name!

Data File

⚲ Thought to be from Toyama prefecture

❀ Thought to be from the Edo period

📖 *Discoveries of the Mysteries of Mt. Tate?!*

✎ Kutahe is the source for the yokai Sukabe introduced on page 68.

Osoresan no Kaicho

A Yokai that appears in a storm!

Data File

- ⚲ Thought to be from Aomori prefecture
- ✲ Thought to be from the Edo period
- ▯ *Encyclopedia of Japanese Phantom Beasts*
- ∥ Winged dragons are called Hiryu or Oryu and can be seen in sculptures and paintings in temples and shrines nationwide.

Surprising!

A friendly prophecy from a terrifying beast!

Hizennnokuni no Icho

Data File

- ⚲ Thought to be from Nagasaki prefecture
- ✲ Thought to be from the Edo period
- ▯ *Encyclopedia of Japanese Phantom Beasts*
- ∥ It's true of all prophetic beasts, but the Hizennnokuni no Icho shows newspapers were willing to print anything that sold.

Looking at it brings lasting happiness?!

The Osoresan No Kaicho, or "Yokai bird of Mt. Osore," is a Yokai that appeared on Mt. Osore in Aomori prefecture. On a stormy day, a strange bird flew out from the dark clouds. It had the face of a person and a body like a winged dragon. It said, "An ill wind will blow next year, killing seventy percent of Japan. Hang my image from your gates to be spared."

Surprising!

Saved by a flying Yokai!

Yokai Prophets

Yogen no Tori

Surprising!

A Yokai that predicted 90% of Japan will die!

Data File

- ⚥ Thought to be from Ishikawa prefecture
- ❈ Thought to be from the Edo period
- 📖 *History of Yamanashi, Historiography, Modern Age*
- 𓏸 The Kumano Gogen are three Shinto Kami considered manifestations of Buddha, enshrined at Kumano Hongu Grand Shrine, Kumano Hayatama Grand Shrine, and Kumano Nachi Grand Shrine.

A sacred crow with two heads

Osoresan no Kaicho has a unique design that printers hoped would be eye-catching to readers.

Hizennokuni no Icho is another prophetic beast that appeared in Hirado, Nagasaki. It manifested as a strange bird, appearing in a flash before onlookers, saying "The new year will see five years of abundance following by plague. Those who see my image will not fall sick and enjoy lasting fortune!"

It then flew off somewhere. Illustrators drew it as a bird with a human-like facial expression.

Yogen No Tori manifested on Mt. Haku in Ishikawa prefecture. It was a bird with two heads.

To the person it appeared before, it prophesized, "Ninety percent of Japan will die in a disaster. If you venerate my image morning and night, this disaster can be averted."

According to the person who recorded this encounter, the Yogen no Tori was a messenger of the Kumano Gogen. Usually, the avatar of this group is a three-legged crow called the Yatagarasu. The Yogen no Tori looks quite different.

References

Ando Seichi, editor. *Researching Wakayama*. Volume 5, Dialects and Folklore Studies. Seibundo Shupan Publishing.

Choshi City Cultural Society, editor. *Folklore of Choshi*. *Choshi* City Board of Education Publishing.

Folk Studies Institute. *Comprehensive Japanese Folklore Vocabulary*. Heibonsha.

Folklore Committee, editor. *Folklore*. Volume 2, Number 6. Hakko Publishing.

Fujizawa Morihiko, editor. *Complete Collection of Discourse* on Yokai Art. Volume 1. Chuo Bijyutsusha Fine Art Publishing.

Fukuda Yoshio, editor. *Supplemented Local Legends of Aichi Prefecture*. Taibundo Publishing.

Hamamatsu City Tachikasai Middle School, editor. *Culture and Climate of Our Kasaichi Town*. Hakko Publishing.

Hiejima Shigetaka and Takezama Yuhi, authors. *Legends of Miyazaki*. Kadokawa Shoten Publishing.

Hino Iwao, editor. *Animal Yokai Collection*. Volume 1. Chuo-koron Shinsha Publishing.

Ibara Kasuo, editor. *Tanuki of Awa*. Educational Center Publishing.

Inada Koji and Hatakeyama Choko, editors. *Folktales and Songs of Hikawa, Izumo*. Techosha Publishing.

Inada Koji and Ozawa Toshio, editors. Survey of *Japan's mukashi banashi*. Volume 21: Tokushima and Kagawa. Dohosha.

Ishigawa Ichiro, editor. *Dictionary of Edo period Literature and Folklore*. Tokyodo Publishing.

Ito Atsushi, editor. *Legends of Japan's Sarayashiki*. Kaichosha Publishing.

Iwata Junichi. *The Ama of Shima*. Nakamura Haruaki Publishing.

Japanese Folklore Academic Society, editor. *Folklore*. Volume 14, Number 5. Hakko Publishing.

Kamigata Kyodo Research Committee, editor. *Local Customs Research, Kamigata*. Volume 33. Sogensha Publishing.

Kasai Shinya, editor. *Tanuki Tales of Awa*. Chuo-koron Shinsha Publishing.

Kenichi Tanigawa, editor-in-chief. *Historical Collection of the Lives of Japanese Common People*. Volume 16. San-ichi Shobo Publishing.

Kinno Seichi and Suchi Tokuhei. *Legends of Iwate*. Kadokawa Shoten Publishing.

Kinoshita Hiroshi, editor. *Encyclopedia of Okayama Yokai*. Nihon Bunkako Publishing.

Koma Toshio and Nakagawa Masafumi, editors. *Legends of Kyoto*. Kadokawa Shoten Publishing.

Kondo Mizuki, editor. *Hyakki Ryoran: Collection of Edo Kaidan and Yokai Picture Books*. Kokusho Kankokai Publication Society.

Konno Ensuke, editor. *Japanese Kaidan Collection, Yokai Edition*. Volume 1. Chuo-koron Shinsha Publishing.

Konno Ensuke, editor. *Japanese Kaidan Collection, Yokai Edition*. Volume 2. Chuo-koron Shinsha Publishing.

Konno Ensuke, editor. *Japanese Kaidan Collection, Yurei Edition*. Shakai Shiso Publishing.

Kotonami City Magazine Editorial Committee, editor. *Stories of Kotonami*. Kotonami City Publishing.

Kyodo Research Publishing, editor. *Local Customs Research*. Volume 5, Number 2. Hakko Publishing.

Kyodo Shumisha Editorial, editor. *Regional Hobbies*, Number 17. Hakko Publishing.

Kyogo Natsuhigo, writer, Tada Katsumi, editor. *Field Guild to Yokai*. Kokusho Kannkokai Publication Society.

Maruyama Mana. *Folktale Collection of Kumamoto Prefecture*. Nihon Dangisha Publishing.

Matsutani Miyoko, editor. *Modern Folktales*. Volume 3. Chikuma Shobo Publishing.

Matsutani Miyoko, Ichihara Rinichiro and Katsurai Kazuo. *Legends of Tosa*. Kadokawa Shoten Publishing.

Momose Meiji. *Kappa Monogatari*. Kawade Shobo Publishing.

Momose Meiji. *Tengu!* Buneido Publishing.

Mori Mashiho, translation editor. *Collection of Ainu Folk Traditions*. Iwanami Shoten Publishing.

Moriyama Taitaro and Kita Josuke. *Legends of Aomori*. Kadokawa Shoten Publishing.

Mt. Tate Museum, editor. *Discoveries of the Mysteries of Mt. Tate?!*. Hakko Publishing.

Murakami Kenji. *A Walk with Japan's Yokai*. Kadokawa Shoten Publishing.

Muto Tetsusho. *Memoirs of an Akita Winter Hunter*. Keiyusha Publishing.

Namazu Meiji Historical Museum, editor. *Illustrated Book of Medical Practices in Numazu in the Early Modern Period*. Hakko Publishing.

Nanto Research Committee, editor. *Nanto Research*. Number 19. Hakko Publishing.

Ono Chuko, editor. *Folklore of Joshu*. Miraisha Publishing.

Oshima Tatehiko, editor. *Kotoyoka – The 8th*. Iwasaki Bijyutsusha fine art Publishing.

Ota Ward Board of Education, editor. *Cultural Properties of Ota – Twenty-Two Collections of Literature and Oral Traditions*. Ota Ward Publishing.

Rokininsha, editor. *Folklore – Traditions and History*. Volume 26, Number 2. Hakko Publishing.

Sangensha, editor. *Travel and Legends*. Volume 8, Number 5. Hakko Publishing.

Sangensha, editor. *Travel and Legends*. Volume 13, Number 5. Hakko Publishing.

Sangensha, editor. *Travel and Legends*. Volume 15, Number 3. Hakko Publishing.

Sano City Historical Society, editor. *History of Sano – Folklore Edition*. Sano City Hakko Publishing.

Sanyo Shinbosha Editorial Department, editor. *Collection of Kibi*, Second Volume. Sanyo Shinbosha Publishing.

Sasaki Kizen. *Kikimimi Zoshi*. Chikuma Shobo Publishing.

Sasaki Kizen. *Zashiki warashi and Oshira-sama of Tono*. Chuo-koron Shinsha Publishing.

Sato Arifumi. *The Most Complete Japanese Yokai Field Guide*. Ribu Shobo Publishing.

Shibata Shokyoku, editor. *Encyclopedia of the Strange and Mysterious*. Chikuma Shobo Publishing.

Shibuya Isao, editor. *Kitsune's Yawn: Folktales of Fujiwara*. Nihon Minwa no Kai Publishing.

Shimabukuro Genshi. *Local Customs of Yanbara*. Kyodo Research Publishing.

Shimano Toshimi, editor. *Folktales of Chiran*. Chiran Board of Education Publishing.

Shiragawa Marina. *Yokai Paradise*. Bestseller Publishing.

Shizuoka Government, editor. *History of Shizuoka Prefecture*. Volume 24, Folktales. Hakko Publishing.

Shizuoka Prefecture Women's School Research Club, editor. *Legends and Mukashi banashi of Shizuoka Prefecture*. Nagakura Shoin Publishing.

Suetake Yoshiichi. *Folk Tales of Ueno and Asakusa*. Sanseisha Publishing.

Suzuki Tozo. *Edo Talk of Fujioka*. Chikuma Shobo Publishing

Tachigawa Kyoshi, revision editor. *Collection of Hyakumonogatari Tales*. Kokusho Kannkokai Publication Society.

Takagi Ichinosuke, collated edition editor. *Heike Monogatari*. Iwanami Shoten Publishing.

Takeda Tadashi. *Legends of Murayama Region of Yamagata Prefecture*. Tohoku Shuppan Kigaku Publishing.

Takehara Shun, artist. *Night Stories of Tosanjin – Ehon Monogatari*. Kadokawa Shoten Publishing.

Tome City Magazine Editorial Committee, editor. *Tome City Magazine*. Tome City Publishing.

Toriyama Sekien. *Toriyama Sekien's Gazu Hyakki Yako Complete Collection*. Kadogawa Shoten Publishing.

Umeki Hidenori. *Legends of Oita*. Volume I. Oita Tosho Publishing.

Wada Hiro, editor. *Kappa Folklore Dictionary*. Iwanami Shoten Publishing.

Wada Hiroshi, editor. *Obake Stories of Kishu*. Meicho Shupan Publishing.

Watanabe Setsuko, editor. *Urban Legends of Okutama*. Aoki Shoten Publishing.

Yamada Norio. *A Journey through Tohoku Kaidan*. Jiyu Kokuminsha Publishing.

Yamanashi Government, editor, *History of Yamanashi*, Historiography, Modern Age. Hakko Publishing.

Yanagita Kunio, Supervisor, NHK Publishing, Editor. *Japan mukashi banashi Memories*. NHK Publishing, Inc.

Yanagita Kunio. *Discourse on Yokai*, New Revision. Kadokawa Arts and Sciences Publishing.

Yanagita Kunio. *Mountain Life*. Kadokawa Shoten Publishing.

Yanagita Kunio. *Tono Monogatari*. Shinchosha Publishing.

Yomiuri Shinbun Hama City Branch Office, editor. *Legends of Kanagawa*. Yurindo Publishing.

Yumoto Koichi, editor. *Encyclopedia of Japanese Phantom Beasts*. Tokyo Bijyutsusha Fine Art Publishing.

Yumoto Koichi, editor. *Field Guild to Yokai*, Continued. Kokusho Kannkokai Publication Society.

Yumoto Koichi, editor. *Teito Yokai Newspaper*. Kadokawa Shoten Publishing.

Yumoto Koichi, editor. *Yokai Hyakumonogatari Emaki*. Kokusho Kannkokai Publication Society.

"Books to Span the East and West"

Tuttle Publishing was founded in 1832 in the small New England town of Rutland, Vermont [USA]. Our core values remain as strong today as they were then—to publish best-in-class books which bring people together one page at a time. In 1948, we established a publishing outpost in Japan—and Tuttle is now a leader in publishing English-language books about the arts, languages and cultures of Asia. The world has become a much smaller place today and Asia's economic and cultural influence has grown. Yet the need for meaningful dialogue and information about this diverse region has never been greater. Over the past seven decades, Tuttle has published thousands of books on subjects ranging from martial arts and paper crafts to language learning and literature—and our talented authors, illustrators, designers and photographers have won many prestigious awards. We welcome you to explore the wealth of information available on Asia at **www.tuttlepublishing.com**.

Published by Tuttle Publishing, an imprint of Periplus Editions (HK) Ltd.

www.tuttlepublishing.com

ISBN 978-4-8053-1723-5

English Translation © 2023 Periplus Editions (HK) Ltd

GAKKARI YOKAI DAIZUKAN
Copyright © 2021 Kenji Murakami
English translation rights arranged with Seibundo Shinkosha Publishing Co., Ltd. through Japan UNI Agency, Inc., Tokyo

Staff (Original Japanese edition)
Illustration Miho Imai, Hidemitsu Shigeoka, Tatta Chabashira
Design Mariko Hyuga (Office Hyuga)
Planning/Editing Mioko Monoga
Proofreading Akaenpitsu

Printed in Singapore   2301TP
27 26 25 24 23   10 9 8 7 6 5 4 3 2 1

Distributed by
North America, Latin America & Europe
Tuttle Publishing
364 Innovation Drive
North Clarendon
VT 05759-9436 U.S.A.
Tel: (802) 773-8930
Fax: (802) 773-6993
info@tuttlepublishing.com
www.tuttlepublishing.com

Japan
Tuttle Publishing
Yaekari Building 3rd Floor
5-4-12 Osaki Shinagawa-ku
Tokyo 141 0032
Tel: (81) 3 5437-0171
Fax: (81) 3 5437-0755
sales@tuttle.co.jp
www.tuttle.co.jp

Asia Pacific
Berkeley Books Pte. Ltd.
3 Kallang Sector, #04-01
Singapore 349278
Tel: (65) 6741-2178
Fax: (65) 6741-2179
inquiries@periplus.com.sg
www.tuttlepublishing.com